THE LAIRD'S YULETIDE BRIDE

❄

BOOKS BY EMMA PRINCE

Highland Bodyguards Series:

The Lady's Protector (Book 1)

Heart's Thief (Book 2)

A Warrior's Pledge (Book 3)

Claimed by the Bounty Hunter (Book 4)

A Highland Betrothal (Novella, Book 4.5)

The Promise of a Highlander (Book 5)

The Bastard Laird's Bride (Book 6)

Surrender to the Scot (Book 7)

Her Wild Highlander (Book 8)

His Lass to Protect (Book 9)

The Laird's Yuletide Bride (Book 9.5)

Book 10 coming 2019!

The Sinclair Brothers Trilogy:

Highlander's Ransom (Book 1)

Highlander's Redemption (Book 2)

Highlander's Return (Bonus Novella, Book 2.5)

Highlander's Reckoning (Book 3)

Viking Lore Series:

Enthralled (Viking Lore, Book 1)

Shieldmaiden's Revenge (Viking Lore, Book 2)

The Bride Prize (Viking Lore, Book 2.5)

Desire's Hostage (Viking Lore, Book 3)

Thor's Wolf (Viking Lore, Book 3.5)

Other Books:

Wish upon a Winter Solstice (A Highland Holiday Novella)

To Kiss a Governess (A Highland Christmas Novella)

Falling for the Highlander: A Time Travel Romance (Enchanted Falls, Book 1)

THE LAIRD'S YULETIDE BRIDE

HIGHLAND BODYGUARDS, BOOK 9.5

EMMA PRINCE

For Scott. Always.

CHAPTER 1

❄

December, 1322
Eilean Donan Castle, Scottish Highlands

For the thousandth time in three days, Fillan MacVale ripped his gaze from Adelaide MacDonnell.

This time, however, he could not credit the force of his will to put an end to his staring. Nay, it was the blast of frosty air from the Mackenzie keep's opening doors that jerked his attention from the bonny lass.

Beside him, Laird Reid Mackenzie shot to his feet and hastily made his way around the long wooden table laden with the Yuletide feast.

"Little Bird!" Reid bounded from the raised dais and wove through the other trestle tables and benches filling the castle's great hall. As the clanspeople at the tables cast their eyes to the keep's double doors, a cheer went up.

A very pregnant young woman filled the doorway, followed by a russet-haired man with a protective arm looped around her back. The woman's gray eyes—Mackenzie eyes—locked on Reid, and a wide grin split her face.

"Brother," she said warmly, embracing Reid.

"We were beginning to get worried, Little Bird," Reid said, setting his wee sister back and assessing her with his sweeping gray gaze.

"Apologies," the man beside the Laird's sister said. He cast a pointed look at the woman's rounded belly. "Our going was a bit…slower than even we anticipated."

Fillan blinked in surprise. The man spoke with an English accent.

The woman rolled her eyes. "My overprotective husband insisted that we only ride an hour at a time, and no more than four hours in a day," she said to Reid. "We wouldnae have missed the first two days of yer Yule festivities if he wasnae so bull-headed."

"Good man," Reid said, turning to the Englishman and extending his hand. "I appreciate yer care with my sister, Beaumore."

The two shared a hearty forearm clasp before Reid turned to those gathered in the hall. "Let us welcome Mairin Mackenzie Beaumore back to Eilean Donan."

Another cheer went up for the Laird's sister.

"And let us also welcome her husband, Niall Beaumore. He may be English, but any man who can capture my wee sister's heart must have the strength and honor of a Highlander."

That was met with laughter and another cheer, along with several raised mugs of ale to toast the impending arrival of their bairn.

"Come, get warm and make yerselves comfortable," Reid said, guiding them toward the dais.

On the other side of Reid's empty chair, Corinne Mackenzie, the Laird's wife, struggled to rise as their newly arrived guests approached.

Fillan shot from his seat to assist her. He winced as his weight came down on his bad foot, but he forewent his cane in favor of leaving his hands free to assist Corinne, who was even rounder with child than Mairin.

"Sweeting, ye neednae—" Reid began, but Corinne was already pulling herself up with the help of Fillan's extended arm.

"I cannot very well greet my beloved sister-in-law from my chair," Corinne retorted.

Letting go of Fillan, she wrapped Mairin in her arms, but the two women's bellies prevented them from being able to properly hug. They both looked down, then broke into laughter at their predicament.

"From your voice, I gather that you are a former countrywoman of mine, Lady Mackenzie," Niall said, giving her a gallant bow.

"Aye, indeed. But please, call me Corinne," she replied warmly. "We are family now."

In response, Niall smiled and tilted his head in acquiescence.

"I want ye to meet Laird Fillan MacVale, Little Bird," Reid murmured to Mairin.

Mairin's gray eyes widened. "Yer—"

3

"Aye," Fillan cut in. He took a hobbling step forward and bowed formally. "Reid's half-brother."

Even three years after first learning of his and Reid's shared blood, saying the words aloud made Fillan's heart jerk against his ribs—in part out of gratitude for the knowledge that he was no longer alone in this world. But not entirely. The shame still lingered. Even in death, Fillan's father cast a long shadow.

When Fillan straightened, he found Mairin's flinty eyes searching him. She took in the MacVale plaid around his hips and his misshapen clubfoot before returning her gaze to his face.

"Ye share Reid's dark coloring," she said cautiously. "And his eyes, though yers are brown."

Fillan gave a single, stiff jerk of his head. "Aye."

While he and Reid had both gotten their nigh-black hair from their shared father, Serlon MacVale, Reid had received the same gray eyes as Mairin and their other brother, Logan, from their mother, Brinda.

That was because Serlon had raped Brinda just before she'd wed Mairin and Logan's father, Laird Murdoch Mackenzie. Brinda had borne Reid, who clearly took after neither flame-haired Murdoch nor sable Brinda. Murdoch had accepted Reid as his own, though, and passed the Mackenzie Lairdship to him as his eldest son.

Serlon, on the other hand, had turned his attention to ravaging more women, including Fillan's long-dead mother. Reid and the others were too polite to speak of it out loud, but from the heavy silence that fell, they were all thinking of the grim history that bound Reid and Fillan together.

"Fillan has been hard at work as the Laird of the MacVales," Corinne said, clearly trying to alleviate some of the awkwardness hanging over them all. "Otherwise you might have been able to meet him earlier, Mairin."

"Aye," Reid added, giving Fillan a nod. "He is building a new legacy for his people."

Tentatively, Mairin reached out and took Fillan's hand. "I am glad to meet ye, then," she said. "After all, ye are my brother's brother. That makes us family—of a sort, anyway."

Fillan dipped his head over her hand, the knots in his chest easing slightly. "Thank ye," he murmured. "It would be an honor to call ye family."

As Serlon's spawn, Fillan knew he didn't deserve to be welcomed by the Mackenzies. Yet Reid had been willing to give him a chance three years past to prove that he wasn't like their father—cruel, manipulative, and greedy. It moved him that Mairin, who wasn't bound by any blood connection with him, would do the same.

"Let me introduce our other honored guest," Reid said to Mairin and Niall, turning to the far end of the table. "Laird Arthur MacDonnell."

Though he'd remained seated through the earlier introductions, the gray-haired Laird now rose and tipped into a bow toward Mairin and Niall. "Pleased to meet ye," he said gruffly as Mairin curtsied and Niall bowed. "And this is my daughter, Adelaide."

Despite his best intentions, Fillan's gaze snapped to Adelaide once more. His eyes would not let go as she rose from her chair and dropped into a low curtsy, her honey-brown head ducked shyly.

"She was supposed to marry the Laird here after my elder daughter passed on," Laird MacDonnell continued, gesturing toward Reid. "But instead he found himself a bonny Englishwoman, and I am back to searching for a suitable match for her."

"Father," Adelaide hissed, casting him a desperate sideways glance as she lifted herself slowly out of her curtsy.

Fillan's fists clenched at his sides. There was no malice in the Laird's blunt words—only thoughtlessness.

MacDonnell had been furious upon learning that Reid had married Corinne three years past despite an informal understanding between the two Lairds. Reid was supposed to have married Adelaide, the younger sister of Reid's first wife. But eventually matters had been smoothed between them. MacDonnell had warmed to Corinne, and the alliance between the Mackenzies and MacDonnells had remained intact.

Still, the Laird spoke without care for the hurt and embarrassment he caused Adelaide—which was obvious from the crimson burn in her cheeks.

Mairin's brows rose at MacDonnell's brusque comment, and Niall cleared his throat.

"Come and sit by me, Mairin," Corinne said. "You must be tired from your travels."

Reid sobered. "Aye, and I wouldnae mind hearing what news ye ken of the Bruce."

As everyone took their seats, Fillan just caught Corinne's whispered aside to Mairin.

"Don't mind Laird MacDonnell. He may be rather rough-edged, but his presence here is important to Reid. He hopes to help the MacDonnells and the MacVales improve their relationship."

It was a noble effort on Reid's part, but Fillan feared it was in vain. While the Mackenzies has entered an alliance with the MacVales almost immediately after Fillan had taken the Lairdship from Serlon, MacDonnell had been far more wary.

He had every right to be, of course. Serlon had spent decades raiding and destroying MacDonnell lands along their border. Neither Fillan's vow to refute his father's ways nor the clan's effort as a whole to right their past wrongs had been enough to convince Laird MacDonnell that things were truly different now.

Apparently this shared Yuletide celebration was meant to bring them together, but as of yet, MacDonnell had barely said two words to Fillan. And for his part, Fillan had been so bloody distracted by Adelaide's shy beauty that it felt as though his wits had been baked into the Yule pudding.

"What news from the Bruce?" Reid prompted again once they were all settled.

Mairin plucked a mincemeat pie from the bounty spread on the table and took a bite.

"Things have been quiet since the Bruce's victory over King Edward at Old Byland Bridge in October," she commented once she'd swallowed. "It seems Edward has completely abandoned the Borderlands for fear of being embarrassed in defeat yet again."

"Which means the Border lords will have to take matters into their own hands," Reid surmised.

"Indeed," Niall said grimly. "In fact, there are rumors that Edward's new favorite, Andrew Harclay, may already be planning to do just that. He is said to be arranging a meeting with the Bruce himself to negotiate a peace."

"Hold there," MacDonnell said from the other end of the table. His bushy brows were lowered and he wore a frown of confusion behind his graying beard. "Wasnae Harclay just made Earl of Carlisle by Edward himself no' long ago? And now the English Earl is in talks with the Scottish King?"

"Harclay's lands are vulnerable so close to the border," Mairin clarified. "Especially now that Edward has ceded the north to us. He has little choice besides going directly to the Bruce for a treaty to protect himself —even though it is treasonous."

"And ye say a meeting between the two is imminent?" Reid asked.

"If the rumors are to be believed, it will happen in a matter of a sennight or two," Niall replied.

"Truth be told, brother, I'd far rather be at the Bruce's side with a sword in my hand in case matters take a turn than sitting on my arse feasting with ye in honor of Yule," Mairin said, casting a sly grin at Reid as she took another bite of pie.

Niall lifted a russet eyebrow at his very pregnant wife. "I think you know I would have a few objections to that, love."

Several at the high table chuckled at that, but despite

the lightened mood, sadness settled like a heavy cloud in Fillan's chest.

Though the Bruce's Bodyguard Corps still operated in relative secret, Fillan knew of its existence thanks to Reid. The team of elite warriors had been assembled to protect those most vulnerable to attack in Scotland's war with England, and to serve the Bruce's cause for freedom more broadly. Both Niall and Mairin were members, and the Bruce had called Reid an honorary member for his work on a mission that had eventually led to his marriage to Corinne.

The Corps represented the sort of principled effort that had inspired Fillan to lead the MacVales toward a new way of life, a better future.

And it was exactly the sort of organization which he would never be a part of. His clubfoot prevented him from ever becoming a truly great warrior. Aye, he could do a bit of training with the men, but even mere walking required a cane. He was proud of his role in bringing the MacVales back in line with the Bruce's cause, but he couldn't shake the feeling that he came short as their Laird. As a man.

Serlon's voice still echoed in his head. *Ye are worthless. A weakling and a cripple. No heir of mine will shame me as ye do.*

His father had valued brute strength above all else— which Fillan had been sorely lacking as a lad with a misshapen foot. Freed of Serlon's cruelty these last three years, Fillan had put his wits and determination to use as Laird, along with the sinewy strength he'd built in his body, but his father's words still lingered in the dark corners of his mind.

His gaze slid to Adelaide once more. She was everything he was not—innocent, beautiful, graceful, sweet.

And she was not for him.

MacDonnell wanted to match her with a Laird, aye, but not the Laird of a clan which he considered more enemy than friend. In MacDonnell's view, the MacVales were still to be watched carefully with a wary eye for any sign of slipping back into their old ways.

But it was more than that. Fillan would never saddle such a woman, who radiated the warmth and light of the sun itself, with the shadows that followed him. He wouldn't be a burden on anyone ever again.

It seemed he was fated to remain close enough to see what he didn't deserve to have. He would simply have to endure this Yuletide with whatever scraps of dignity he could salvage.

CHAPTER 2

Adelaide simply had to endure this Yuletide with whatever scraps of dignity she could salvage.

She sat quietly as the others spoke around her, keeping her gaze fixed on her entwined fingers resting in her lap. Outwardly, she fought to show no sign of her mortification. But inside, a tempest of hot humiliation lashed her.

It had been bad enough that her father had forced her to accompany him to the Mackenzies' Yule feast. She had naught against Laird Reid Mackenzie and his lovely wife Corinne. In fact, she admired the clever, warm Englishwoman. And it was plain to see that she and the Laird were fiercely in love.

But being at Eilean Donan only reminded her of her sister's death—and the embarrassing arrangement that had followed.

Dear, sweet Euna had been like a second mother as well as a sister to Adelaide. Their mother had died when

Adelaide had been just five. Twelve-year-old Euna had taken responsibility for Adelaide's upbringing while their father led the clan through many years of turmoil with the MacVales.

To seal an alliance with the Mackenzies, Euna and Reid had been wed. But less than two years later, Euna lay cold in the rocky Highland ground, along with the bairn she'd carried. She and the unborn babe had been poisoned in a scheme to fan the flames of discord between the MacVales, Mackenzies, and MacDonnells.

It had been a terrible blow to lose her sister. But worse, her father had pressed the idea that when she came of age, Adelaide ought to take Euna's place as Reid's wife.

Though Reid was a handsome man and the Laird of a large and powerful clan, the thought of marrying him had curdled Adelaide's stomach. He was only a few years shy of having two decades on her in age. But more than that, in her mind he was her brother-in-law —*family*, not a husband.

Her father, of course, hadn't listened. She couldn't truly be mad at him for that—after all, the safety and wellbeing of the MacDonnell clan as a whole was more important than the feelings of one lass. So in the few years that Reid and her father had agreed to wait while she came of age to wed, she had done what she could to prepare herself for the union.

Her relief had far outweighed the prick to her pride in being passed over when Reid had abruptly married Corinne. Still, it had stung somewhat. First she had been little more than a replacement for her sister, and then she had been set aside all together.

It had been awkward enough to come to the home of the man she'd been meant to marry and his charming, beautiful wife, but Adelaide had managed to plaster on a smile for the Yule festivities. Yet when her father spoke so baldly of her position as his unwed, passed-over daughter, she wanted to melt into the rushes underfoot.

And he'd done so in front of everyone. In front of *Fillan*.

She dared a glance at the MacVale Laird from beneath her lashes. His dark brows were drawn together, as if he were concentrating on the conversation flowing around the high table. Yet his eyes, which appeared nearly black in the warm light filling the hall, drifted absently over the spread of goose, bannocks, meat pies, roasted vegetables, and puddings covering the table.

His lips naturally curved upward at the edges, as if his mouth were made to lift in mirth, yet in the last three days of feasting and celebrations, Adelaide had not once seen him smile.

Nor had he so much as grinned when he'd visited the MacDonnell keep three years past to formally sign a treaty with her father, plus a few times each year since then to discuss the MacVales' progress of making amends to the MacDonnells. Nay, from the moment she'd laid eyes on him, he'd borne a furrowed brow and a frown.

It was plain to see that he was a serious man, despite only being a small handful of years older than Adelaide. She supposed that at only twenty herself, she ought to find him rather stodgy and grim, but instead she found herself curious about his solemn nature and drawn to the quiet dignity in the set of his mouth and the serious cast of his gaze.

Just then, those lustrously dark eyes lifted to her. Barely managing to suppress a gasp of surprise, Adelaide jerked her gaze back to her lap. Heat crept up her neck and into her face. She prayed that he wouldn't notice her blush, but his keen eyes never seemed to miss aught.

"I don't mean to interrupt," Corinne said, catching a lull the discussion of politics and war. "But we needn't spend the entire evening speaking on such grave topics. This is Yule, after all."

"Ye're right, of course," Reid said, brushing a tender kiss on Corinne's cheek. "Ye ought to eat yer fill in peace, Little Bird, Niall. And mayhap ye'll wish to rest after yer travels."

"Nay!" Mairin replied. "We only just got here, and this is Yule, as Corinne says. Might we dance to a carol?"

Corinne clapped her hands. "Oh, that would be wonderful!"

"Are you sure that's wise?" Niall asked Mairin, frowning.

Mairin rolled her eyes, but she gave Niall a half-grin. "It's only a wee bit of dancing."

"If I can do it, Mairin certainly can," Corinne proclaimed, rising from her chair.

"Easy, lass," Reid said. He took her elbow, helping her to her feet.

When he laid his other hand on her rounded belly, Adelaide's heart gave a pang of longing. Not for Reid, but for what he had. A family of his own. A beloved partner. A second bairn on the way to join their first, who had long since been taken to bed by a maid.

Once Corinne was on her feet, she called for the musicians in the opposite corner of the hall to strike up a carol. Clanspeople, who were finishing their meal at the trestle tables below the dais, shouted and clapped with excitement. They leapt into action, clearing the benches and tables to the sides to make room for dancing.

As was traditional, they began to form a circle, waiting for the minstrel singer and the pipes and drums that accompanied him to begin the song. Someone even threw open the hall's double doors, letting in a whoosh of bracing air to cut the roaring heat of the blazing Yule log in the hearth.

Niall and Reid both lifted their wives, round bellies and all, down from the dais, but Mairin hesitated as they turned to gather with the others.

"Would ye like to join us, Adelaide?"

Warm gratitude filled her at Mairin's kindness, yet it was surpassed by a wave of embarrassment at being the center of attention for a moment.

"I-I have no partner," she murmured.

"Cannae ye solve that, Fillan?" Mairin asked, casting a questioning look at the MacVale Laird.

For one breathless moment, the thought of dancing with Fillan made Adelaide's heart go still in her chest.

But when her gaze snapped to him, his eyes were pinched with pain and a muscle in his jaw ticked.

"I cannae," he replied lowly. "My foot doesnae allow for dancing."

Now it was Mairin's turn to flush. "Och, aye. Apologies."

Fillan waved her off, but Adelaide didn't miss the way his throat bobbed with a tight swallow.

"Ye can still join us, Adelaide," Corinne said, giving her a smile. "It is a circle dance, not a paired one."

When Adelaide hesitated, Corinne went on. "Come. It's Yuletide, and as your hostess, I insist that you enjoy yourself."

There was no arguing with that, so Adelaide rose and stepped from the dais to follow the others. It might have been her imagination, but the tingle between her shoulder blades told her that Fillan watched her go.

When she reached the circle of eager clanspeople, she wedged her way in, linking elbows with Mairin and a tall, barrel-chested Mackenzie man who only had eyes for the woman on his other side.

The minstrel sang out the first note, then the pipers and drummers joined him. With a cheer, the circle of dancers began to revolve, their steps matching the drummers' rhythm.

From the weave of the others' feet, Adelaide recognized the dance. She followed the patterns adeptly, stepping into the circle with the other women, then moving back out as the men did the same, then clapping twice with everyone before joining elbows once again.

At last, she let herself be at ease, losing her nerves and embarrassment in the flow of the cheery dance.

But just as they began their final rotation, the minstrel broke off the song long enough to call out, "Watch where yer menfolk are leading ye, lassies!" He pointed to the great hall's rafters, where a bundle of mistletoe had been hung amongst the evergreen boughs in honor of Yule—right over the dancers.

That was met with a roar of laughter and a few shouted jests about more bairns being added to the clan soon.

As a man and a woman rotated under the mistletoe, they broke from the others, turned to each other, and the woman planted a hearty kiss on the man's grinning mouth. They moved into the middle of the circle, clapping and cheering as the next couple shifted into the gap they'd left beneath the mistletoe.

Pair by pair, each couple kissed and moved into the middle, making room for more lovebirds to meet under the mistletoe. Belatedly, Adelaide realized that only Reid and Corinne and Niall and Mairin stood between her and dreaded public humiliation. She tried to unhook her elbows, but the man beside her had his arm locked and his head turned toward the lass on his other side.

Reid and Corinne shared a swift but sweet kiss, much to the approval of their clanspeople. Niall and Mairin lingered a moment longer, drawing a few good-natured ribs. Then suddenly, Adelaide stood beneath the mistletoe.

Alone.

One of the pipers missed a note. An older clansman,

clearly into his cups, asked loudly where the MacDonnell lass's partner was. Luckily, Adelaide didn't hear the response, for her pulse pounded deafeningly in her ears. She went hot all over, and her throat closed so tightly that it felt as though she couldn't breathe.

Someone nearby said something to her, but instead of turning to see who spoke, she ducked her head and darted from beneath the clump of mistletoe. With her eyes on the floor and her heart racing with humiliation, she didn't know which way to go. Her feet carried her toward the open hall doors, seeking the relief of the frosty, dark night.

Once she was outside, she broke into a run, the hot tears slipping from the corners of her eyes turning to cold daggers against her cheeks.

CHAPTER 3

F or a terrible heartbeat, Fillan forgot about his damned foot. He forgot that he was a MacVale and Adelaide a MacDonnell, and that he wasn't supposed to want her.

All he knew was that she had been caught alone below the mistletoe in front of at least a hundred people, most of them strangers.

He jerked to his feet, his chair scraping over the dais. As if he could save her, like some gallant hero from a storybook. Half a breath later, reality came crashing back. His weight landed on his bad foot and he grunted in discomfort. He would have wobbled and mayhap even bumped into the table if his cane hadn't been close at hand.

Laird MacDonnell rose too, a frown on his face.

"Oh dear," Corinne said, waddling to the dais. "I should have anticipated that for Adelaide's sake."

"She's always been a lass of feeling," MacDonnell

said gruffly. "I'll see to her and make sure she doesnae work herself up and make matters awkward."

Fillan barely managed to bite his tongue to keep from pointing out that it was MacDonnell who was far more likely to cause a scene when it came to his daughter.

Corinne's thoughts seemed to run in the same direction. "Mayhap you ought to give her a few moments alone instead," she suggested gently. "This entire visit must be a bit uncomfortable for her, what with…" She waved broadly to take in the whole situation.

"It isnae as though she can truly leave, nor will she be in any danger," Reid added, coming to Corinne's side. "One of many benefits of having an island keep— no one comes and goes on a whim."

MacDonnell grunted and lowered himself into his chair once more. "Aye, I suppose ye're right. Besides, I wanted to talk to ye about the forested land along our border, Mackenzie. The deer herd there seems to be thinning, and—"

"I think I'll take some air as well," Fillan blurted.

He should have kept his mouth shut and sat with Reid and MacDonnell to discuss deer—or aught else that would help improve the bonds between their three clans. But an image of Adelaide, red-cheeked and head lowered, fleeing the keep, was burned onto his mind. MacDonnell may think his daughter was just being silly, but Fillan had seen true pain on her face before she'd slipped out.

Reid raised a dark eyebrow at him and Corinne's eyes widened at his proclamation. MacDonnell didn't acknowledge that Fillan had spoken at all, so he limped from behind the table and off the dais, heading for the open doors.

He instantly wished he'd brought his cloak, for the air was sharply frigid outside. At least he had an extra length of green and brown MacVale plaid slung over his shoulder.

He quickly scanned the courtyard, but all was still. His gaze rose to the battlements on top of the curtain wall surrounding the keep. On the side closest to the shore, he made out a few shadowy figures in the guard-house, but elsewhere the battlements were empty. It seemed that Reid had given most of the guards permission to join the festivities inside, leaving the battlements quiet besides the few left keeping watch on the shore.

Just then, his gaze snagged on a slash of light blue against the inky black night.

Adelaide. She stood on the battlements opposite the guardhouse, overlooking the spreading sea-loch on the other side of the island castle. Her pale gown rippled softly in the slight breeze coming off the water.

As if he were being pulled by an invisible string, he found himself walking toward her. He had to lean heavily on his cane as he made his way up the battlement stairs, but he hardly noticed the usual discomfort in his foot, for his attention was fastened on her.

Her back was turned, her slim shoulders caving in and her arms clutched around her middle. So as not to startle her, he cleared his throat when he reached the top of the stairs.

At the noise, her head snapped around. Her soft

chestnut eyes were wide with surprise—and bright with tears.

Fillan swallowed, his tongue suddenly turning to a wooden block. "Forgive the intrusion," he said at last. "It was warm in the hall and I…I thought to get some air."

"A-aye," she replied, turning back to the dark water to hide her face. "So did I."

"Ye've picked a fine place to do it," he said, taking a step toward the edge of the battlements.

He leaned one shoulder against the top of the wall, propping his cane against the stones. The land to the north and east, and in the distance to the south, was dusted with snow that appeared blueish white in the dark. But both the water and the sky were an inky black, pinpricked with silvery stars and their reflection. It was impossible to tell where the sky ended and the water began.

It was beautiful, but Fillan found his gaze sliding to her. Only then did he realize that she was shivered.

"Ye're cold," he said, silently berating himself for not noticing immediately.

She began a weak denial, but he yanked the plaid from his shoulder and had it draped around her in a heartbeat.

Belatedly, he realized that they now stood so close that their frosted breaths mingled between them. He fiddled with the edges of the plaid, trying to tuck them in without touching her. Yet it was as if his hands had a mind of their own, for they would not cease their task for another long moment.

At last, he managed to jerk his hands to his sides. He

clenched them into fists against the desire to reach for her.

"I'm sure ye noticed what happened in there," Adelaide said with a forced huff of air that sounded like an attempt at a chuckle. "I am fine, I assure ye. Ye neednae stand out here in the cold just because——"

"Would ye prefer to be alone?"

Her eyes jolted to his. Her lips opened and closed before she could form a reply. "Nay," she murmured at last.

"Then I dinnae mind being out here. In fact, I prefer it to sitting in the hall."

She swallowed. "It was silly of me to leave, I ken. But..." Her voice tightened until it approached the breaking point. She seemed to decide something then, for she turned to him, staring up with soft, vulnerable eyes. "But have ye ever felt as though ye were all wrong? No' the situation, no' everyone else, but *ye*?"

The breath left Fillan's lungs on a hard exhale. "Aye."

Her brows notched together in cautious surprise. "Ye have?"

"I ken that feeling verra well." Absently, he squeezed his right thigh, which had drawn tight with exertion in compensation for his foot. "Ye ken something of my family? Of my father?"

"Aye," she replied hesitantly. "He was a warmonger."

"And a cruel bastard. He thought beating me would toughen me up, though no matter how many times he kicked or hit, it never straightened out my foot."

A sharp breath of air puffed in front of her lips. "I am sorry."

"He is gone now." Fillan didn't say that Serlon still cast a long, dark shadow over his life. No need to saddle her with his sad history. But he needed her to know he understood. "It is remarkable how much a father can make ye feel unwanted, though."

He cast her a searching glance. Her own father's tactlessness in speaking of the broken marriage alliance between her and Reid seemed to play a large part in her embarrassment, along with the reminder she'd received under the mistletoe that she was unwed. But Fillan wasn't sure if there was more to it—including possible unreturned feelings for Reid, her former intended.

"My father isnae a tyrant," she replied, then quickly added, "No' to say that—"

"Nay, no need. My father *was* a tyrant," Fillan said. "I am glad yers isnae."

With a swallow, she tried again. "He isnae cruel, only unthinking at times. And no' of the clan. It is his duty to put the wellbeing of the entire clan first. Sometimes that means putting his daughter last."

"Ye mean the fact that ye were supposed to marry Laird Mackenzie?"

She nodded wordlessly.

"And ye…ye were disappointed that ye didnae?" he asked cautiously.

"Nay!" she blurted, turning round eyes on him. "I was disappointed that they planned such a thing in the first place. Reid was my sister's husband, and the thought of marrying him after her death…"

She shook her head and hunched into Fillan's plaid. "I am happy for Reid and Corinne," she continued. "But to be here is a reminder that I havenae found my own place yet. My father still hopes to marry me in a good match—good for the clan, of course. Until he finds someone suitable, I am to remain the second daughter, the passed-over bride."

Fillan's heart squeezed at that. It was a relief to hear from her own lips that she harbored no lingering feelings for Reid. But the idea that this beautiful, sweet-natured woman felt out of place and unwanted was unaccept-able. Especially when *he* wanted her so damn bad.

She looked out at the black water once more, sighing ruefully. "I tried to avoid coming here altogether, for I didnae want to be a reminder—to Reid, to Corinne, or my father—of the past arrangement. But my father thinks I need to toughen a bit, especially if I am to become the lady of another clan's keep soon."

"Take it from me," Fillan murmured. "The world toughens us enough. We dinnae need our family taking the task on for themselves."

"Aye," she said quietly, then huffed another sad chuckle. "At least that scene under the mistletoe wasnae his doing. Nay, that was all me, making a fool of myself. Now I am no' only the discarded bride, but also the daft MacDonnell lass who's never even been kiss—"

She cut herself off with a breath, her eyes flying to Fillan for an instant before jerking away. Even in the low light, he could see her cheeks flush.

Heaven help him. She had likely only meant to say that she hadn't been kissed that night, in front of everyone.

Yet it seemed she'd accidentally confessed to never having been kissed at all.

"Would ye…" Damn it all, now his tongue had its own mind along with his hands. He couldn't seem to stop the words from slipping out. "Would ye like to be kissed?"

A voice screamed at him from the back of his head. He was mad. He was daft. He was approaching something dangerously enticing, like a moth to a flame. Yet he couldn't take back the words now. The breath froze in his lungs as he waited for her reply.

She darted another wide-eyed look at him, but this time her gaze lingered. It traced over his face and across his chest and shoulders before settling on his mouth.

"Now? Here?" she breathed.

"Would ye rather go back to the hall? The mistletoe will still be—"

"Nay!" She clamped her mouth shut, swallowing. "That is, I dinnae wish to be amongst a crowd. But…we are alone now."

Good God, was this truly happening? Would he be Adelaide MacDonnell's first kiss, out here beneath a sparkling winter sky?

He felt drunk at the possibility, yet he knew the heady feeling didn't come from whisky. After seeing his father overindulge nearly every day, Fillan had vowed never to do the same. Still, the feeling of intoxication at the prospect of kissing Adelaide was more potent than any drink.

She looked up at him, uncertainty making her shy.

Yet her gaze no longer wavered. In fact, her eyes were filled with curiosity and...dare he call it longing?

Fillan snipped the bud of hope in his chest then. Aye, she felt longing—to experience her first kiss, naught more. Not longing like he felt for her—a bone-aching, gut-twisting yearning that had seized him from the moment he'd laid eyes on her three years past and had only grown stronger over time.

He would give her this, an experience she could remember later with a wee smile or a chuckle at the silliness of it all. She would know that she was desired, wanted, and would no longer have to fret about that first press of lips again.

It wouldn't mean to her what it meant to him. But as long as he was gentle, made it pleasant and sweet, she wouldn't have to know about the need that burned beneath his skin.

"Ye are sure?" he murmured, taking a half-step closer.

When she nodded, her lips parting on a misty breath, his heart leapt into his throat. An instant later, he closed the rest of the distance between them.

CHAPTER 4

Adelaide's breath hitched at Fillan's nearness. She had to tilt her head back to hold his dark gaze as he moved so close that only a whisper of cold air separated their bodies.

This is madness. She shouldn't even be speaking to him, unaccompanied and in the dark, let alone agreeing to a kiss. But the prospect of those curving yet serious lips brushing hers kindled a fire deep in her belly that could not be doused with rational thought.

He dipped his head toward her, but then he froze, lingering only a few inches away. It seemed this would not be the swift, congenial kiss she'd seen so many couples exchange. Nay, Fillan apparently wanted to draw out the moment, his gaze intent as he traced her features.

Her pulse sped from a trot to a gallop. Did he find her lacking? Was that why he hesitated? Suddenly uncertain of herself, she sank her teeth into her lower lip, as if to hide it from his dark, unreadable eyes.

As though he feared spooking her, he lifted one hand and cautiously cupped her flushed cheek. Despite the heat in her face, his palm, roughened with calluses, was warmer. His thumb settled on her chin. Gently, he pried her lip from between her teeth.

Cold air whispered across her dampened lip for a heartbeat, and then his mouth was on hers.

Everything seemed to fall silent then. Even her heart missed a beat, leaving one long, quiet instant in between its swift hammerings.

Though his lips were so often set in a steady, serious line, they were shockingly soft and warm. His hand slid to the back of her neck, his fingers threading through the hair there and holding her in place gently.

At first, his mouth barely brushed hers, sending matching flutters into the pit of her stomach. But then Fillan pressed more firmly, and the butterflies turned into ribbons of fire. He tilted his head so that their lips fitted together in an intimate embrace, her lower lip nestling between both of his.

Adelaide had no sense of how much time had passed, but when Fillan shifted, she assumed it was to put an end to their connection. Without thought, she pressed closer rather than drawing back, unwilling to lose the heat of his lips just yet.

But to her satisfaction, he didn't pull away, either. Instead, he placed all his weight on his good foot, then leaned his shoulder against the stones rising from the battlements. Without his cane in hand, he'd likely grown uncomfortable standing. But rather than end their kiss, he'd found a way to extend it.

As he continued to move his lips slowly over hers, brushing then pressing, tilting his head to catch every angle, her mind began to spin. To steady herself, she slipped one hand from the folds of the plaid he'd spread around her and placed it on his chest.

It was as if her light touch broke a dam. He made a sound in the back of his throat that sounded half-pained, half-hungry. His fingers tightened in her hair, sending prickles of sensation over her scalp and across her skin.

To her shock, the velvet heat of his tongue flicked against her lips. Tentatively, she parted them. His tongue slipped inside, finding hers and caressing it.

Good gracious. This was astoundingly intimate, so much more than she could have imagined. Their lips fused together as their tongues tangled in a dance that implied acts well beyond her experience.

And it wasn't just their mouths. His fingers sank into her tender nape—a place no man had ever touched before. His scent, of smoke and soap and male skin, enfolded her, clinging to the plaid around her shoulders and filling her nose. And the heat of his body—it radiated from him as if he were a blacksmith's forge.

Beneath her hand, the linen of his shirt was hot. His heart pounded, swift and erratic, just below the surface. He was surprisingly hard, his sinewy strength making his chest feel like a stone wall.

The man kissing her was Fillan MacVale, yet this was a side of him she'd never witnessed before. In place of his usual controlled, solemn demeanor was a man of scorching flesh and rushing blood. A man of passion and urgency. Of commanding need.

Her mind simply couldn't make sense of the blazing reality of this moment. So she surrendered to sensation, riding the rising wave of her own need. She curled her hand into his shirt, trying to pull him impossibly closer. Her tongue matched his strokes, deepening their entanglement.

"...been too long." A voice drifted up from the courtyard below the battlements. "I'd best ensure the daft lass hasnae frozen solid."

A *familiar* voice.

Through the haze of mounting desire, an alarm bell clanged in Adelaide's mind. But her body was sluggish and warm with pleasure. She couldn't seem to reason out what she ought to be doing instead of kissing Fillan.

"What the bloody..."

Her father. He'd been the one who'd spoken a moment before. He was in the courtyard. And he'd seen them.

Too late, the pieces came crashing together and Adelaide's wits rushed back. At the same instant, she and Fillan jerked apart.

"MacVale!" Laird MacDonnell roared. Like a charging bull, he barreled across the courtyard and up the stairs to the battlements.

Abruptly, Fillan jerked her behind him, positioning himself between her and her father. He took a hobbling half-step to square his shoulders to the enraged Laird as he reached the battlements.

Distantly, Adelaide realized that Fillan thought to protect her from her father's anger. Of course, her father would never strike her, even in a fury like this one, but Fillan didn't know that. He only had his own father to go from. His protective impulse made something in her heart fracture, and a flood of warmth filled in the cracks.

"MacVale, ye bloody, stinking—" her father bellowed.

"Let me explain, Laird," Fillan said, his voice surprisingly calm.

Her father jabbed a finger into Fillan's chest. "No need. I saw enough with my own eyes. Ye have sullied my daughter, ye cowardly, deceiving—"

This time Adelaide was the one to cut off her father's rant. She stepped around Fillan's broad shoulder and faced him.

"Nay, Father. Fillan didnae—"

"Och, so he is *Fillan* to ye now, daughter?" he snapped.

"He didnae sully me," she continued, resolutely holding her chin steady. "I allowed him to kiss me."

Her father turned a dark red behind his beard. "Nay. I dinnae believe that. Besides, ye are little more than a bairn, Adelaide. Even if this bastard didnae force ye, he clearly manipulated ye."

"I didnae force yer daughter, nor did I manipulate her," Fillan said stiffly. "It was an innocent kiss, meant only to soothe her pride after what happened in the hall."

Adelaide's stomach dropped. Was that all it had

been to him? A wee kiss to placate her, like a sweet given to a bairn who'd skinned her knee?

She ducked her chin, feeling small and foolish for having imagined so much more in their kiss. It was happening again. She wasn't wanted. Not truly. She was only a sad lass to be taken pity on.

"I'd sooner eat my boot than believe the lies of a MacVale," her father replied heatedly to Fillan. "Ye will pay for dishonoring my daughter, I vow——"

"What goes on here?" Reid said from the keep's open doors.

"MacVale has assaulted my Adelaide," her father replied loudly, uncaring of the curious faces peering out from the great hall behind Reid.

Reid hurriedly crossed the courtyard and climbed to the battlements.

"There must be some misunderstanding," Reid said, keeping his voice low as he eyed each one of them in turn.

"Aye," Fillan said, but before he could explain further, Laird MacDonnell jumped in again.

"I saw him with my own eyes," he said again, jerking his finger at Fillan. "He had my daughter pressed against the stones like some common whore!"

"I kissed her, aye," Fillan said to Reid. "But I didnae coerce her."

"The hell ye didnae!" her father roared. "First I witness ye treating her like a whore, and now ye are *calling* her a whore, as if she would so wantonly invite yer touch."

"No one is saying—" Reid began, but her father plowed on.

"I should never have turned my back on ye, MacVale," he hissed. "I kenned yer promises of turning over a new leaf were too good to be true. My instincts were right about ye. Ye are conniving and manipulative, trying to take advantage of an innocent for yer benefit— just like yer father."

Adelaide sucked in a cold breath. Beside her, Fillan jerked as if her father had just landed a punch to his chest.

"Enough," Reid barked. Clearly fighting for composure, he smoothed a hand over his dark hair. "Mayhap we'd best continue this discussion someplace more *private*," he said pointedly to MacDonnell.

Adelaide's gaze slid to the still-open keep doors. To her horror, several dozen people now stared at them, and the music from deeper in the hall had died. She was the center of attention again, in the worst possible way.

Her father had apparently noticed their audience, for he huffed a breath. "Aye, verra well."

"Come," Reid said to all of them. "Let us sort this out in my solar."

CHAPTER 5

Fillan trailed behind Reid, MacDonnell, and Adelaide. Blessedly, Reid kept his pace slow enough that Fillan could keep up. But it made their crossing of the great hall long and uncomfortable.

The tap of Fillan's cane on the ground was the only sound at first. But then the whispers began. There was no avoiding the stares, either, for MacDonnell had assured with his shouted accusations that even from all the way on the battlements, everyone in the hall had heard.

As they headed toward the stairs, Corinne started to rise from her seat on the dais, a question in her eyes for Reid.

Reid held up a hand to stay her. "All is well," he said to both Corinne and everyone else. "Only a wee misunderstanding to smooth out. Please, all of ye, carry on with the celebrations."

Still, the murmurs and stares followed them. In front

of him, Adelaide hunched in on herself, her head tucked and her shoulders slumped. Belatedly, he realized she still wore his clan plaid. No doubt none in the hall had missed that.

From the bright color on the one cheek he could see, she likely wished to flee the hall once more. But her father had her arm tightly tucked under his so that she couldn't escape.

At last, they reached the shelter of the stairs. They climbed one flight to a landing bearing two doors. Reid took the one on the right, which opened to a tidy solar.

As Reid hastily lit the fire that had been laid in the hearth, Fillan took a moment to glance at the room. A large wooden desk, along with a few cushioned chairs, dominated most of the open space. The top of the desk was covered in parchment and writing supplies. Corinne, who served as the clan's scribe and record keeper, undoubtedly used the space more than Reid, yet the tapestries, the heavy wooden furniture, and the large hearth had a more masculine feel.

"Sit," Reid ordered once the fire flared to life. They each took a chair except for Reid, who perched on the edge of the desk. "Now, explain what happened— without shouting," he said, pinning MacDonnell with a look before turning his attention to Fillan.

"I found Lady Adelaide on the battlements," Fillan began. "She was cold, so I gave her my plaid. We talked. It seemed she was distressed at being caught under the mistletoe alone, so I…" He swallowed. God, what an idiot he'd been. "I offered to kiss her."

"And I agreed," Adelaide added, her gaze darting to

her father before returning to her lap.

"I willnae hear this," MacDonnell grumbled. "Mac-Vale is up to something, I ken it. If he didnae force her, then he has some scheme in mind—to ruin her marriage prospects by sullying her good name, mayhap, or—"

Fillan gripped the arms of his chair to keep from pounding a fist against them. If he lashed out now, he would only be proving MacDonnell's words—that he was no different than Serlon MacVale.

Blessedly, Reid cut MacDonnell off before he could spew more venom.

"Fillan has no reason to do that," he said evenly. "These past three years, he has proven to the Macken-zies that he means to keep his word and lead the MacVales in a new direction. He and his people have also worked to make amends to the MacDonnells, isnae that right, Laird?"

Grudgingly, MacDonnell gave a single, curt nod.

"Then why would he jeopardize all that hard work over a single wee kiss?"

Why, indeed? Damn it all, Fillan hadn't been thinking of the lace-thin alliance he was supposed to be strengthening when he'd kissed Adelaide. He'd only been thinking of easing her hurts—and, if he were honest, indulging in an intimacy he'd dreamed of for three long years.

"I dinnae ken the nature of his schemes," MacDon-nell replied, "but he is a MacVale. He no doubt seeks some benefit in smearing my daughter's prospects."

"That is what ye're worried about?" Reid asked. "Adelaide's marriage prospects?"

"Aye, and her good name. The clan requires her to make a useful match. No self-respecting man will have her if he kens that some MacVale dallied with her first."

Reid frowned at that, but his gaze drifted from MacDonnell to the fire. For a long moment, the only sound in the solar was the crackle in the hearth.

"I wonder…" Reid said, glancing from Adelaide to Fillan.

Though he didn't know his half-brother well enough to read his slate-gray eyes, the hairs at the nape of Fillan's neck pricked with some intuition of impending danger.

"What are ye about, Mackenzie?" MacDonnell demanded warily, clearly sensing the same thing.

Deciding something with a nod to himself, Reid focused on MacDonnell once more.

"I have the solution to yer problem, and a way to advance the trust and goodwill between the MacVales and the MacDonnells."

A heartbeat before Reid spoke, realization dawned on Fillan.

Bloody hell.

"Fillan and Adelaide shall be married," Reid finished.

"Nay," Fillan said flatly even before the last word was out.

"What?" MacDonnell snapped.

Fillan dared a glance at Adelaide. Her head snapped up and her eyes went wide with shock for a fleeting moment, but at Fillan's swift refutation, her brows crumpled together and she dropped her gaze to the floor.

"Hear me out," Reid said to MacDonnell, ignoring Fillan. "If they marry, there are no prospects to ruin, no sullying of the lass's name, naught untoward for the gossips to latch onto. And ye said ye wanted an advantageous match, MacDonnell. What could be more advantageous than a neighboring Laird, one who could shore up an alliance between yer clans to everyone's benefit?"

"But dinnae ye see, Mackenzie? He is scheming something, just like Serlon would ha—"

"I would remind ye," Reid cut in, his voice hard as granite, "that ye are speaking of *my* father as well as Fillan's. Ye are also casting aspersions on a Laird with whom *I* am allied. Mayhap ye'd best cool yer temper before ye say something that threatens the valuable relationship the Mackenzies and MacDonnells share."

That had MacDonnell sitting back in his chair, his lips clamping shut at last.

"I didnae mean to dishonor Adelaide in any way," Fillan said, taking the opportunity to speak. "Nor am I plotting aught to harm her or yer clan, Laird. Ye ken I have done all in my power these last three years to show ye that I am in earnest when I say I wish to make peace with ye." Fillan swallowed. "But," he continued. "I cannae marry yer daughter."

"Why no'?" MacDonnell demanded. It seemed the man was prepared to take offense no matter what Fillan said, but at least he was no longer shouting.

"Aye," Reid asked, frowning. "What objection could ye have?"

Fillan felt Adelaide's eyes on him, but he willed himself not to look at her. The last thing he wanted to do was hurt her. She'd already known the sting of rejection, and she didn't deserve more of the same.

Yet to marry her would be to burden her with a crippled husband, not to mention a Laird who was still struggling to rebuild his clan and atone for the sins of his father. He would not yoke her to his hardscrabble life, no matter how badly he longed to hoard her light and grace for himself.

"It would...no' be an agreeable match," he replied after a moment. Not agreeable for *her*, he thought.

"Ye seemed plenty agreeable when ye had yer mouth on her," MacDonnell retorted.

But Fillan ignored him, instead turning his gaze to Adelaide. She still had her chin tucked, but now a bright slash of red marred her creamy cheeks, as if she'd been slapped.

Damn him. No doubt she imagined he meant that he found *her* disagreeable, which couldn't be farther from the truth.

But he couldn't let his desire to alleviate her discomfort in the short-term outweigh his concern for her well-being in the long-term. She was young, vibrant, and beautiful, the embodiment of grace and sweet innocence. Being saddled with a husband like him would crush the light in her, scrub away all the softness like so much grit trapped against delicate skin.

"What if I sweetened the arrangement?" Reid persisted, still frowning at Fillan. "Mayhap fifty head of cattle to each clan? Call it a wedding present."

That got MacDonnell's attention. "It means that much to ye, does it, Mackenzie?"

"I would like to see Fillan wed, aye," he replied. "And Adelaide, for I ken the fact that she is unmarried is my doing. But most of all, I wish to have peace between our clans—no' this half-peace laced with wariness and distrust, but a true union to benefit us all."

MacDonnell eyed Fillan then. "How can I be expected to trust my only daughter to a MacVale?"

"Ye ken I vouch for Fillan," Reid cut in. "He is a good and honorable man. No harm would ever come to Adelaide under his care."

That much Fillan could wholeheartedly agree with, but he was still gripped with the conviction that forcing him and Adelaide into a marriage would be ruinous.

"I must object—" he began, but MacDonnell cut him off, turning back to Reid.

"I'll hold ye to that. Both of ye." He spared Fillan a brief, withering look before fixing Reid with a hard stare once more. "And I'll expect those cattle come spring, no later."

"Father, nay," Adelaide said, her voice thin. "If Fillan doesnae want to—"

"This isnae about wanting or no' wanting, girl," MacDonnell interjected sharply. "I dinnae want to wed ye to a MacVale, that's for damn sure, but here we are. Mackenzie is right. This will save yer reputation and the MacDonnell clan name. And while I willnae be holding my breath for a stronger alliance with the MacVales, the gifted cattle will help our clan."

He turned narrowed eyes on Fillan. "And believe me, I will be watching ye, MacVale. Do wrong by my Adelaide, or by the MacDonnells, and so help me—"

"It's settled, then." Reid clapped his hands, cutting off MacDonnell's threat. "Fillan and Adelaide shall be wed as soon as possible."

Bloody hell. This was happening. Judging from the way MacDonnell set his jaw, there would be no further chance to convince him to call this off.

"Unfortunately, the Mackenzie priest is laying Auld Rabbie Mackenzie to rest a day's ride from the keep," Reid continued. "Otherwise I'd urge ye to speak yer vows tonight."

"So soon?" Adelaide breathed.

Fillan's stomach sank. She was clearly resistant to this union as well. After all, why would she want to be bound to a cripple for the rest of her life?

"There is a priest at the MacVale keep," he said woodenly. "Though if Adelaide wishes to delay—"

"Och, nay ye dinnae," MacDonnell growled. "I see what ye are about. Ye think ye will find a way to weasel out of this with a wee bit more time, and let the gossip of what ye did on the battlements spread. Come first light tomorrow morn, we will ride to the MacVale keep and I will ensure with my own eyes that ye make an honest wife of my daughter."

"But Father," Adelaide said. "What of my things? My clothes? They are all at our keep. Couldnae we go there first for a few sennights, or even a few days so that I can prepare?"

Fillan's heart joined his stomach on the floor. Since she couldn't stop this disaster of a marriage, she was trying to put it off as long as possible. Aye, she'd been willing to share her first kiss with him earlier, but that didn't mean she'd be eager to accept a deformed husband.

Yet it seemed both their fates were sealed now.

"Nay," MacDonnell said flatly. "Tonight is all ye'll have. Come, daughter. Ye'd best get what rest ye can."

MacDonnell rose and stiffly extended his arm to her. Reluctantly, she took it, letting him pull her to her feet and toward the door. She kept her gaze downcast the whole time, never meeting Fillan's eyes.

When the door closed behind them, Reid clapped Fillan on the shoulder.

"Felicitations. I only regret that I willnae be able to see ye wed myself, for I am loath to leave Corinne so close to her time, and she is in no state to travel."

"Why did ye do that?" Fillan ground out, barely managing to keep his temper in check. He rose to face his half-brother. "She doesnae deserve to be saddled with the likes of me."

Surprise flashed in Reid's gray eyes for an instant before being replaced with understanding.

"I've seen the way ye look at her, lad," he replied quietly. "But also the way she looks at ye. I think if ye give it a chance, ye might find that ye are both well pleased with the match."

Fillan fumbled for a reply, a way to refute what Reid had said, yet he found his tongue was a useless knot.

"Come," Reid said, patting Fillan's shoulder again. "Let us return to the festivities. Corinne will want to hear the happy news."

And with naught else left to do, Fillan grudgingly followed him out of the solar.

CHAPTER 6

D espite the clear blue sky overhead and the brilliant sun, which reflected nigh blindingly off the snow, Adelaide drew her hood more fully over her head.

She could claim that it was only to ward off the nipping cold as they rode to the MacVale clan keep. But the truth was, she wanted to block Fillan from the corner of her vision. And hide her burning cheeks.

For once, though, her blush wasn't out of excitement at his nearness. Nay, humiliation made her face hot despite the frosty air.

He didn't want her. It had been plain the moment Laird Mackenzie had suggested that she and Fillan wed.

Aye, he hadn't minded sharing a kiss when there had been no one to see, but at the prospect of marrying her, he'd blanched and his hands had turned to white-knuckled knots. And he'd spoken swiftly and decisively against the union. Clearly, he wanted this as little as her father did.

What a fool she'd been. For an instant on the battlements, she'd thought he felt the same flutter of warmth and weightless stomach as she did whenever he was near. And when he'd kissed her... It showed what a silly, naïve lass she was that she thought the heat they'd shared had meant something more.

That morning, as they'd been rowed to the mainland and retrieved their horses from the stables that served Eilean Donan, he hadn't even been able to look at her. It seemed now that he was to be saddled with her, he found her lacking or repugnant in some way.

For her part, her eyes had tugged toward his darkly handsome features as they'd cut northeast across the winter-blanketed landscape. In spite of his sudden frosty distance, she couldn't deny that she still felt drawn to him.

But could she ever let herself care for him as her husband, given that he'd only agreed to marry her under duress? Could their marriage be happy despite the painful knowledge that she was yet again the unwanted bride?

She was left to her churning thoughts most of the day, for no one in their party seemed inclined to speak. Fillan was silent except for a few curt orders to the dozen or so MacVale warriors who'd comprised his retinue to Eilean Donan. And Adelaide's father held his tongue, as did their own handful of MacDonnell men. For several hours, the only sound was the crunch of snow beneath the horses' hooves.

As the winter sun began to make its short descent in the southwest, Fillan cleared his throat and spoke at last.

"The MacVale clan keep is just there." He pointed northward as they crested a small rise.

Sure enough, a dark mass of stone rose from the white landscape in the distance. Behind it, Adelaide noticed a cluster of thatch-roofed huts—the keep's village.

"Ye dinnae have a curtain wall," her father huffed. "How do ye expect to keep my daughter safe without an outer wall?"

"When Serlon was in power, he didnae think we required one—his idea of defensive measures was to always remain on the attack," Fillan replied tightly. "When I became Laird, I considered building one, but with limited resources and manpower, I decided it was more important to mend relations with our neighbors— ye and the Mackenzies. Only once we have fully recovered from the destruction wrought by my father will we begin building a curtain wall."

Her father's bushy gray eyebrows lifted in surprise at that. "Aye, well…" he began, but didn't bother finishing. It seemed that for the first time, he didn't have a cutting word about the MacVales on the tip of his tongue.

As they approached the castle, Fillan lifted his fingers to his lips and whistled loudly. The portcullis began to lift with a groan, and behind it, the castle's wooden gate was ratcheted open. When they crossed through the gate and into the small courtyard, Adelaide could feel several curious stares following them from the battlements.

The castle's single, four-storey tower loomed over

her as they reined to a halt. The keep's doors opened and a round, short woman with an apron tied over her simple brown wool gown bustled out.

"Welcome back, Laird," she said, wiping her hands on her apron. "We werenae expecting ye for another day or t—"

The woman squinted at the large group filling the narrow courtyard, seeming to notice the strange faces among the MacVales for the first time.

"My plans...changed, Gretha. May I introduce Laird Arthur MacDonnell and his daughter, Lady Adelaide. Laird, this is Gretha, who not only runs the keep's kitchens, but also serves as a chatelaine of sorts for the whole castle."

Adelaide dipped her head to the woman, and her father grunted in acknowledgement. For her part, Gretha dropped into a deep curtsy. "My Laird, my lady," she said. But when she straightened, her confused brown eyes sought Fillan.

"Please see that Laird MacDonnell's warriors are given refreshments along with our men," Fillan instructed. "And I ken ye dinnae have much notice, but..." He faltered, flexing his hands on his reins for a moment. "But do what ye can to prepare a feast for this eve. A wedding feast."

"Laird?" Gretha gasped, her eyes darting from Fillan to Adelaide.

"Aye," he said in confirmation. "I am to wed Lady Adelaide. Today. If ye can spare a moment, alert Father Dorian as well. The ceremony will commence in an hour's time, with a celebration to follow."

Fillan's words must have carried, for a surprised ripple of murmurs traveled through the men on the battlements overhead. For her part, Gretha stood in stunned silence for a long moment before shaking herself and dashing inside to see to her long list of tasks.

Ignoring them all, Fillan dismounted. He came down on his good leg before prying his cane from his saddlebags, where he'd tucked it at the start of their journey.

Adelaide unhooked her leg from the saddle's pommel, intending to see herself to the ground, but to her surprise, Fillan moved quickly to her side. Propping his cane against his good leg and leaning one side against the horse's shoulder, he reached for her and lifted her down with startling ease.

When she was on her feet, she dared a glance up at him. His brows were lowered and his eyes were unreadable as he traced her face with his gaze for one lingering heartbeat. All too quickly, he released her and turned away, leaving her to wonder yet again what it was about her that had made him so distant.

"Come," he said over his shoulder to her and her father. "Let me show ye the keep."

Once they'd stepped inside, Adelaide let herself absorb the space. The doors opened to a small but tidy great hall. It was mayhap half the size of Eilean Donan's hall, and smaller than the MacDonnell keep's hall as well.

It also bore none of the festive decorations that the Mackenzie keep had. No evergreen boughs covered the mantel, nor did an enormous Yule log burn in the single hearth. And, Adelaide noted with relief, there was no mistletoe hung overhead.

"Please forgive the lack of embellishment," Fillan said, his voice stiff with discomfort.

It was true. Even setting aside the lack of Yuletide adornment, it was a rather sparse and plain space. The walls were bare of colorful tapestries, and the tables and benches that had been pushed to the sides for the day were simply hewn. Even the furniture on the raised dais along the back wall was carved without flourishes.

"Though we have had two strong harvests since I became Laird, our stores had grown dangerously low under my father's control," he continued. "It seemed best to focus on the fields to ensure that all in the clan had full bellies through the winter rather than use those hours on ornamental weaving or carving to satisfy pride alone."

But despite the unadorned hall, the rushes underfoot were clean and sprinkled with dried herbs, a neat fire was laid in the hearth, and the unlit candles and torches lining the bare walls were all trimmed and well-tended. It might be plain, but clearly the MacVales took pride in tending their keep. As did their Laird.

"And of course we have wished to see that our debts have been paid and restitutions made to our neighbors before turning our attention to non-essential ornamentation," Fillan added, his gaze flicking to her father.

Adelaide knew something of the arrangement between their clans. When Serlon MacVale had been Laird, he hadn't bothered to farm his own lands. Instead, he'd sent war parties to raze and steal in both

MacDonnell and Mackenzie territory. Crofts had been burned, cattle and sheep reived, and crops plundered before being destroyed.

When Fillan had become Laird, he'd agreed to return his people to the hard work of farming and raising livestock on their own land. What was more, he'd also pledged to rebuild every croft that had been damaged and return the animals that had been stolen, or replace them with healthy yearlings. And he'd promised to give a third of the entire clan's harvest to his neighbors to make amends for all the damage his father had done.

It had clearly meant that his own people had been forced to live sparely, yet it seemed they didn't mind, for Fillan had restored honor to the MacVale name. Or at least he was trying.

For his part, Adelaide's father still didn't seem convinced. He grunted noncommittally in response to Fillan's words.

"The wedding is to take place within the hour?"

"Aye. Gretha can show ye to the guest chambers if ye wish to rest and refresh yerselves beforehand," Fillan said.

As if summoned by her name, Gretha appeared in a door at the back of the hall that Adelaide assumed led to the kitchens.

"Gretha, would ye see our guests to the chambers abovestairs? And attend Lady Adelaide in her wedding preparations."

Gretha dipped into a curtsy, then shuffled toward them. "Come Laird, Lady Adelaide."

She whisked them up a narrow, winding staircase, halting on the third storey, where a handful of doors angled out from a landing. She guided Adelaide's father into one, assuring him that a lad would come to light the fire in the hearth and bring refreshments shortly. Then she motioned Adelaide toward another door.

It opened onto a chamber that reminded her of the great hall—sparse, small, yet tidy. A dressing table and chair, a tall armoire, and a bed were the only furnishings. As Adelaide stepped inside, a thought struck her. She wouldn't ever use this bed, for come that evening, she would be wed to Fillan MacVale.

A mixture of fluttering anticipation and knotted trepidation warred in the pit of her stomach. Could he come to care for her, despite the circumstances under which he'd been induced to wed her?

She already knew she was capable of developing feelings for him. Heavens, she already had. He was serious and hard-working, dedicated to those under his care, and honorable to the core.

It would only take a small sign of affection from him to have her tumbling completely over the edge toward love. But likewise, any indication of hesitation or apathy on his part would crush the delicate wings of emotion unfurling in her heart.

Gretha seemed to sense Adelaide's nerves, if not the feelings behind them. She patted Adelaide's hand kindly. "Dinnae fash, mistress," she said softly. "The Laird is a good man. We in the clan have longed to see him wed, and ye seem a sweet-natured lass. Ye have naught to fear in this marriage."

Adelaide's eyes pricked at Gretha's unexpected gentleness. "Thank ye, Gretha. It is only that it's all happening so quickly. I havenae had a chance to—" *To learn if Fillan truly wants me, or is only accepting me because he must.*

She swallowed the words, not wanting to turn to a blubbering mess in front of the keep's head cook and chatelaine less than an hour before her wedding. Adelaide would be the lady of this castle come evening. She had to start on the right foot.

"Aye, well, everything's a wee bit rushed," Gretha said with a chuckle. "But we'll make the most of the time we have to get ye gussied up before yer vows, mistress."

"I...I dinnae have aught else to wear." She cast a glance at her robin's egg blue gown. Blessedly, it hadn't been terribly spoiled by her travels, but it was undoubtedly plain.

"Then we'll make do," Gretha said matter-of-factly. "Ye are a bonny thing, mistress. A bath, a combing, and some fresh plaits in yer hair, and ye'll be polished up to glowing, ye'll see."

With that, Gretha poked her head out the door and called for a tub and hot water to be hauled up, quick as the servants could manage.

CHAPTER 7

For the dozenth time, Fillan caught himself tapping his cane on the outside of his bad foot. He planted the cane firmly onto the dais, resolving yet again not to let his nerves get the better of him.

But he had been standing on the dais beside Father Dorian for what felt like an age. It couldn't have been more than a quarter hour, in truth, but time seemed to stretch, taunting his worry-knotted mind.

The great hall was filled with a surprising number of MacVale clanspeople. It seemed word had spread quickly that their Laird was to be wed. They, too, had begun shifting restlessly. They eyed the handful of MacDonnell warriors who stood stoically in their midst, clearly eager to be done waiting.

What if she doesnae come?

Fillan was being foolish and weak-minded, he knew, yet he could not stop the thought from surfacing.

When he'd helped her down from her horse in the

courtyard, he'd felt her tremble slightly. Was she afraid of him? Afraid of what it would mean to marry him? Mayhap she was repulsed by him, and she'd shuddered at his touch—and the prospect of sharing so much more in the marriage bed.

Aye, and mayhap she would find a way to convince her father to call off this madness. Mayhap she was speaking to him at this moment, pleading not to be married off to a cripple, or weeping at the thought of having to endure the sight of his mangled foot for the rest of her life. Mayhap—

Just then, a swell of murmurs rose at the edge of the crowd closest to the stairs. His clanspeople parted, and there she was, descending like a swan.

Her arm was looped with her father's. The Laird wore a frown, but he appeared more baffled than angry at the prospect of escorting his only daughter toward her wedding.

Fillan only spared him a glance before shifting his gaze back to Adelaide. Her hair had been partially pulled back and plaited so that the braids formed a honey-brown crown around her head. The rest of her locks fell in a rich cascade down her back.

There were no flowers to be had at this time of year, but some thoughtful servant—Gretha, most likely—had gathered together a bundle of ribbons that had been tied to look like blossoms. Adelaide held the bunch of colorful ribbons in a hand that shook slightly.

She wore the same light blue wool gown as she had before. No jewels sparkled at her neck, nor had she been bedecked in fine silks and brocades.

She didn't need any of that. Unadorned, her pure, glowing beauty shone like a candle in the dark. She was the most arrestingly beautiful sight he had ever seen.

Distantly, he registered the murmurs of pleasure and awe traveling through the hall as she made her way slowly toward him. It seemed his people were as taken with his bride as he was.

As she and Laird MacDonnell drew closer to the dais, she kept her head modestly dipped. MacDonnell halted at the base of the dais, releasing her arm and placing a peck on her cheek. He cast a lethal glance at Fillan before helping Adelaide step up to his side.

When he took her hand from her father's and guided her before the priest, only then did she lift her eyes, soft as a doe's, to him. She was nervous. He saw it in her gaze and felt it in the tremor of her hand.

The knowledge of her trepidation sank like a stone in Fillan's stomach. Of course she was afraid. Today would mark a turn in her life, binding her to a man who was warped, both inside and out, by the darkness of his birthright.

He had been alone for so long. His mother, who was said to be a kind, gentle soul, had died giving birth to him. And until three years past, he'd had no knowledge of his half-brother Reid. All he'd had in the whole world was a cruel, menacing father who'd bent Fillan to his will with brute force.

He'd been born with a deformed foot. Still, it seemed almost a sign of the warping his soul would undergo beneath the boot heel of Serlon MacVale. For though the man was dead, his words still haunted Fillan.

He was weak. Unworthy. Worthless.

How could he expect aught but Adelaide's revulsion and distress at being yoked to him?

As Father Dorian began the ceremony, Fillan stood woodenly next to Adelaide, her hand still lifted in his but only the pads of his fingers touching her. They each said their vows, their voices drifting over those gathered. When it came time to place a ring on her finger, he produced a simple golden band that had once belonged to his mother and slid it in place.

"Ye may now kiss yer bride."

Father Dorian smiled at Fillan, but it took a moment for his words to sink in.

A murmur of anticipation stole over those gathered. Fillan met Adelaide's gaze. A blush bloomed in her cheeks as she waited, her deep brown eyes revealing uncertainty.

Shameful fear spiked in his veins then. What if she truly was dismayed at having to marry him? What hope could they have for a happy future if she found him lacking, or worse, revolting?

He would never force his affections on her. If it was his misshapen body that offended her, he would simply have to keep his distance, never letting his own longing for her go untethered.

His decision made, he ducked his head toward her. But instead of taking her lips with his, he bowed over her hand. He brushed a kiss onto the cool metal of the ring he'd just placed on her finger, hoping the gesture appeared like a gallant display of his commitment to the vows they'd just made.

But his lips also grazed one of Adelaide's soft, warm knuckles. He straightened so as to break the contact. Adelaide gasped, her eyes rounding, then her brows pinching together in distress.

If she had so strong a reaction even to a glancing touch, what must she feel at the prospect of the marital bed they would share later that night? The thought made Fillan's heart wither inside his chest. He wouldn't terrorize her nor coerce her into accepting her role as his wife. Nay, he would rather sleep in a cold, empty bed for the rest of his life than hurt her in any way.

The gathered MacVales clearly found the peck he'd placed on her hand disappointing. A weak applause rose, but no cheers or shouted felicitations joined it.

Still, he'd made the right decision, he told himself grimly, if her reaction to the brush of his lips on one knuckle was any indication.

This cold union would test him like naught before, but he vowed silently to keep his distance. For her sake.

CHAPTER 8

"I must admit, MacVale. I am…impressed."

Fillan was jerked from his dark thoughts later that evening by MacDonnell's grudging words.

"It seems ye lead a hardscrabble but happy lot of MacVales here," he continued, looking out at the merry gathering in the hall. The tables and benches had been pulled out and a simple feast of roasted meat, vegetable stew, fresh bread, and plenty of ale and wine lay before them.

For all the clanspeople's revelry, however, the high table had been somber and mostly silent all evening. Fillan sat between MacDonnell, who'd held his tongue until now, and Adelaide, who sat rigid and still as a stone statue on his other side.

"Aye," he said to MacDonnell, his thoughts returning to Adelaide once more.

But it seemed that with a full belly, MacDonnell's tongue had loosened. "No' that I trust ye completely," he added. "But now that I see with my own eyes that the clan has come together to embrace a path of honor…"

Fillan tried and failed to focus on MacDonnell's words. They were important, he knew, for MacDonnell was finally warming to him, which meant a more meaningful peace could be on the horizon for their clans. Yet he couldn't stop his gaze from drifting to Adelaide.

From the tightness around her eyes to the stiffness of her shoulders, he suspected that he'd done something wrong. More likely, she was nervous about what lay ahead of them that evening.

As MacDonnell paused in his musings about the MacVales to take a sip of wine, Fillan took the opportunity to lean toward Adelaide.

"I have already spoken with Father Dorian," he murmured, quiet enough for only her ears. "He understands ye are a shy maiden. There willnae be a bedding ceremony."

Even without the taut unease hanging between them, he would have seen that the bedding ceremony be called off. Their consummation—if it were to ever happen—would be a private matter between himself and Adelaide.

"And…" He hesitated before continuing, but the memory of her trembling hand and the way her eyes had clouded when he'd kissed it returned, urging him on. "And dinnae fash over consummating our vows this eve—or ever."

Her gaze snapped to him, Confusion filling her eyes. "What?"

"We neednae…join physically. I will honor ye as my

wife in every way, and no doubt will ever fall on ye, but we dinnae need to become...intimate."

Some unreadable emotion flooded her eyes for a heartbeat before she lowered her head. Fillan would have assumed to see relief there, but it looked strangely more like...hurt.

"Aye," she whispered, her gaze fixing on her knotted fists in her lap. "If that is what ye wish."

Once again, the fleeting feeling that he'd done something wrong rippled over his skin, but before he could analyze it, a voice rose from one of the tables below the dais.

"What's this I hear from Father Dorian?" One of the MacDonnell warriors, a hulking block of a man, rose from his seat. "There isnae to be a bedding ceremony?"

Those around him made good-natured objections, which brought a lopsided grin to the MacDonnell warrior's face. "It is tradition, is it no'?"

Fillan had anticipated this. Once the revelers got into their cups a wee bit, there would naturally be some protestations about curtailing the ancient tradition of the guests carrying the bride and groom to their bedchamber, then waiting outside—probably banging on the door and shouting encouragement—until the groom emerged to chase them all away.

When a caring husband opted to shield his modest bride from the tradition, he was expected to make a concession—to throw one of the bride's stocking garters to the crowd, thus satisfying their enthusiasm for a wee taste of the impending bedding while protecting the bride from further embarrassment.

He looked askance at Adelaide, who nodded almost imperceptibly. A roar of approval went up among the crowd, and the tables were hastily cleared to make room for the guests who would vie for the scrap of material, which was said to bring good luck.

"Is it no' also tradition that the bonny bride give whoever secures her garter a kiss?" the MacDonnell warrior asked, much to the amusement of those gathered.

"Careful, Hagen," Laird MacDonnell growled from the dais. "My daughter may be a MacVale now, but she is still a lady. It is tradition for her to give her *favor* to the man who prevails—she will choose what that is."

The warrior, Hagen, wasn't apparently dissuaded by his Laird's words. He and several of the other MacDonnell warriors crowded into the space in the middle of the hall that had been cleared, each elbowing each other for the best position. More than a dozen unwed MacVale men joined them, jostling with the genial edge that came to the surface when men competed.

Fillan pushed his chair back. Then, with the help of his cane, he lowered onto one knee before Adelaide. He looked up and caught her eye, waiting until she gave another small nod before reaching for the hem of her dress.

As his hand disappeared beneath the wool, several of those gathered shouted bawdy encouragements, making the others laugh and cheer their Laird onward.

He tried to avoid touching her, but when his fingers

brushed her stocking-covered calf, Adelaide jerked. Silently cursing himself, he ventured higher, until he passed her knee. Then he couldn't help but lay a gentle hand on her thigh in order to find the garter.

She stiffened again at his touch, and he glanced up to find her face blazing with a flush, her eyes averted. Loathing himself for making her endure his attentions, however brief, he made quick work sliding the garter down her leg.

When the scrap of embroidered ribbon appeared from beneath her skirts, the crowd roared and called out their support for the waiting bachelors.

Fillan hoisted himself to his feet by his cane. Lifting the garter, he tossed it out into the cluster of men.

They were surprisingly rowdy as they scrambled to secure it. Thomas, the MacVale blacksmith, dove forward to catch it, but no sooner had his hand closed around the bit of material than a MacDonnell elbowed him in the stomach and snatched it from him, much to the crowd's entertainment.

"Ye ken what is also tradition…" Laird MacDonnell watched the mock battle unfold, but he spoke to Fillan. "They say that when the husband is the one to secure his bride's garter, it is a sign that he will remain faithful to her." MacDonnell's gaze slid to Fillan, one of his brows lifted.

It was clearly a challenge. A test. And not just to prove that Fillan would keep his word to be a devoted and committed husband to Adelaide, but that he would remain true in his dealings with MacDonnell as well.

Damn it all. Fillan would never be able to compete

with the braw warriors jockeying in the hall given his clubfoot. He was no warrior-Laird, and he never would be.

But he had to at least try. It would be a way for him to show Adelaide that even though he may be physically malformed, he would always strive to be an honorable husband to her.

As he awkwardly stepped from the dais, Hagen managed to wrestle the garter from one of his fellow MacDonnells. A MacVale tried to seize it from him, but Hagen, who stood a head above even the biggest among the men, batted the man away like little more than a midge.

The crowd applauded, seeming to accept Hagen as the victor, but the cheers began to die down as Fillan approached slowly.

Hagen turned to eye him as he hobbled closer. "Can I help ye, Laird MacVale?"

"Aye. Ye can give me my wife's garter. Or I can take it from ye."

That earned a rumble of approval from the MacVales in the hall.

Hagen, however, was unimpressed. "I have never struck a Laird, nor have I stooped to beating cripples. I dinnae wish to start either now."

At that, Fillan's step faltered. He ground his teeth as disbelieving murmurs traveled over those gathered. It was no secret that his foot was misshapen. But all in the clan knew not to comment on it. His people understood it was a sore spot for him.

Fillan had worked hard never to show feebleness

before the clan. His father had engrained a fear of weakness too deeply in him to root out. He could not simply stand aside now and let Hagen claim victory over him.

"Come, Laird," Hagen said, his coarse features curving in a smile. "Let me have a wee kiss from yer bride. Ye neednae embarrass yerself by trying to fight me. And I promise to be gentle with her."

Och, Fillan was going to best him. And he would enjoy it.

Fillan shuffled forward until he was just beyond Hagen's long-armed reach—but close enough to touch Hagen with his cane if he stretched out. A little space cleared around them, as if all those watching sensed that this was more serious that the earlier good-natured scramble for the garter.

There was no way he could beat Hagen with brute force alone. He was no match for the giant warrior physically. But years of suffering under his father's cruel reign had taught Fillan the value of using his wits over mere brawn. When Hagen impatiently waved Fillan on, he'd already formed a plan.

Bracing both legs, Fillan made as if to swipe a hand at the scrap of material in Hagen's grasp. Hagen lifted his fist high, easily avoiding Fillan's grab. Yet in doing so, he left his middle exposed.

With a swift jab, Fillan drove the end of his cane into Hagen's stomach. The giant wheezed in surprise and doubled over. Fast as lightning, Fillan spun his cane and cracked Hagen over the knuckles with the wood. Hagen hollered, his hand reflexively opening.

The bit of fabric fluttered to the ground between them.

While Hagen fought to regain his breath and nurse his sore knuckles, Fillan bent and scooped up the garter. When he straightened, he brandished the cane in front of him like a longsword in case Hagen thought to retaliate, but the warrior held up his hands in surrender.

"Ye win, Laird," he said with another grin, though now it was rueful rather than arrogant.

This time when those gathered roared their approval, it was so loud as to be nigh deafening. Fillan turned and made his way back toward the dais to return the garter to Adelaide. He found her wide-eyed gaze locked on him as he approached, her lips parted and her cheeks flushed.

"Kiss!" someone shouted from the crowd.

"Aye, kiss yer bride, Laird!"

"Give him a kiss, milady!"

To Fillan's surprise, Adelaide held up a tentative hand. Instantly, the hall fell silent to hear her.

"I will honor tradition and give a favor to the victor," she said. "He may claim a kiss...if he wishes to."

Her gaze ducked from his then, and her cheeks grew even rosier.

Bloody hell. If *he* wished to, she'd said. She would acquiesce to this public display, but from the burn in her face and her downcast eyes, she wasn't doing so willingly.

His mind raced for a way to give her an out.

"I stole a kiss from my lady wife before we were married," he said slowly, loud enough for all in the great hall to hear. He held up the garter, then bowed, extending it toward her and placing it on the dais at her feet. "Let my thievery be forgiven and my debt wiped clean with this."

At least he'd saved her this time from having to kiss him in front of everyone in the clan.

His people were clearly disappointed, for they grumbled quietly about his chivalrous gesture. He ignored them, for only Adelaide's comfort mattered. If their displeasure was necessary for her peace of mind, so be it.

But when he caught her eyes, expecting to see relief, he found them brimming with tears instead.

"P-please excuse me," she mumbled, shooting to her feet and rushing toward the stairs.

Fillan stared after her as she fled, utterly baffled. He'd done everything he could to ease her discomfort at the prospect of being married to him. Yet he'd still managed to fail her somehow.

MacDonnell chuckled softly, drawing his attention. "Verra well fought, MacVale, and well won. Hagen's hand will be sore for a sennight. Mayhap that will give him pause with that overly bold tongue of his."

Fillan nodded in acknowledgement, but he only gave the Laird half his attention as he struggled to understand where he'd gone wrong with Adelaide.

"Ye seem determined to be a good Laird—and a good husband," MacDonnell continued grudgingly. "But take a wee bit of advice from me when it comes to Adelaide."

Fillan's head snapped to MacDonnell then.

"Though she seems quiet as a church mouse, she is prone to strong emotions," MacDonnell said, waving at the stairs where she'd just vanished. "As her father, I tried no' to overindulge her, to prepare her to serve her clan—and the clan she married into. Ye are her husband now, and the responsibility will fall to ye to toughen her up to face the realities of leadership. If I were ye, I'd let her have her cry and then get on with the task of accustoming her to the real world."

"She doesnae need toughening."

Belatedly, Fillan realized that he'd practically spat the words. But the events of the last two days had worn him down enough that he didn't care. Mayhap tomorrow he would regret speaking to his father-in-law and a neighboring Laird so, yet he couldn't stop himself from continuing.

"Nor does she need to be hardened to the harshness of life. She is perfect the way she is. In fact, I'm going to fight tooth and nail to keep her soft and spoiled for the rest of her life. I *treasure* the fact that she has a gentle soul and a tender heart. I wouldnae dream of changing—"

Suddenly, realization hit him like a bucket of ice water to the face.

Fearing her rejection, he'd turned hard with her. Distant. Cold. Like her father. Like *his* father.

If he truly meant all he'd just said, he couldn't allow his own worries to destroy his delicate bride. He needed to fix this—*now.*

Without hesitation, he headed for the stairs, ignoring MacDonnell's flabbergasted harrumph and the stares of his clan as he went.

CHAPTER 9

Adelaide needed to get away from here—from the keep, from the eyes of the crowd, and most of all from this cold, unhappy marriage.

When she reached the stairs, her feet carried her to the guest chamber Gretha had shown her to earlier. But when she pushed inside, the chamber was dim and empty.

Gretha had said that she'd send word down to the stables to have Adelaide's saddlebags and the few possessions they contained brought up to her chamber after the ceremony. Belatedly, Adelaide realized that this was no longer considered her chamber. She was supposed to share with Fillan now.

But judging from the way he'd treated her ever since that blasted kiss on the battlements at Eilean Donan, he would want her to remain as far away from him as was possible in the small castle.

On wooden legs, Adelaide descended one flight of

stairs to the door Gretha had indicated was Fillan's. The chatelaine-cook had pointed it out when they'd been making their way to the hall for the wedding ceremony.

The door swung open on well-oiled hinges. Someone had thoughtfully lit the fire in the hearth in anticipation of the newlyweds' arrival. A large bed sat against the back wall, a trunk at its foot. There was a writing desk beneath the shuttered window, and an armoire with a smaller table containing a bowl and pitcher beside it.

The faint scent of smoke and soap and clean masculine skin hung in the air—Fillan's scent. The space was as sparse and serious as the rest of the keep, yet it felt lived in. She could almost picture Fillan seated at the desk, his handsome face set in lines of concentration. Or leaning back against the carved headboard, the blankets bunched around his trim waist…

She jerked her thoughts away from the tempting image. He'd made it clear that he wanted naught to do with her. And she couldn't stay and wait as her heart slowly withered and died, knowing he'd only married her because he'd been trapped. Knowing he would never truly want her.

Her saddlebags had been propped against the chest at the foot of the bed. But her cloak was nowhere in sight. Resolutely, she moved to the armoire and pulled open one of its doors. Neat rows of plain shirts and MacVale plaids hung inside, and the scents of soap and Fillan were stronger here. Steeling her heart, she shuffled through them until she found her cloak hanging at the back.

She hastily slung it around her shoulders and crossed to her saddlebags. She had no idea what she'd do next. To get out of the keep, she'd have to cross through the great hall, which was packed with clanspeople. Still, she closed the leather flaps on the bags and cinched them tight.

But just as she was about to hoist them up onto her shoulder, the chamber door opened.

When Fillan stepped inside, taking in the scene with unreadable eyes, the breath froze in her lungs.

"What are ye doing?" he asked quietly.

"I…" Adelaide willed herself to lift her chin and meet his gaze. "I am leaving."

He closed the door behind him but remained where he was, his brows lowered and his mouth tight.

"Where?"

"To a nunnery. I…I think we ought to get an annulment. I'll take my vows to God so that my father doesnae have to worry about my future marriage prospects, and ye can continue with yer life here."

"Is that…" His throat bobbed as he swallowed. "Is that what ye want, then?"

She felt her face warming. It was a half-formed plan at best, but aught was better than being the unwelcome and unwanted wife for the rest of her life.

"I think it is best." She took a deep breath to fortify herself for what needed to be spoken next. "As ye said, this is clearly no' an agreeable match. It seems there isnae room in yer life…" She pushed past the knot rising in her throat. "…Or in yer heart for me. I dinnae wish to burden ye with—"

"What?"

At the sharply spoken word, her head jerked up, but she found his dark brows winging with perplexity.

"Ye think ye are…" He raked a hand through his hair. "Ye are *far* from a burden to me, Adelaide. And ye've already claimed a place in my heart."

Now it was her turn to go wide-eyed in confusion.

"I dinnae understand. Ye spoke against our union. And ye've made it plain that ye dinnae wish to touch me. Ye wouldnae kiss me during the wedding ceremony, nor when ye won the garter. And ye have made arrangements to ensure that…" Her face went hot. "…That we dinnae make this a *true* marriage."

Fillan squeezed his eyes shut, shaking his head slowly. "Bloody hell. What a mess I've made."

When his eyes opened, he fixed her with a desperate, searching look. "I only thought to save ye from my attentions if they werenae welcome. I felt ye tremble when I helped ye down from yer horse and thought ye found my touch…disagreeable. I tried to spare ye, both during the ceremony and just now in the hall, from having to bear my kiss."

She ducked her head, her fingers fiddling with each other. "If I seemed displeased, it was only because I am shy—and saddened to realize that ye arenae happy to have been forced into this marriage."

"Is that what I've made ye think? That I didnae want ye?"

She nodded, no longer trusting her voice to escape past the pinch in her throat.

He moved toward her then—cautiously, as if

approaching a wounded animal. "Naught could be further from the truth, Adelaide. The fact is, I have been dunderheaded over ye since the moment I saw ye three years past. Do ye remember the night? Yer father asked me to ride to the MacDonnell keep to sign a peace accord on behalf of the MacVales. Ye were seated beside him on the dais, wearing a crimson gown that made yer skin look like cream."

The breath left her in a hard exhale. Could this be real? "A-aye, I remember."

"Ye were all eating yer evening meal, but once I signed the accord, yer father didnae invite me to stay and dine with ye. He wanted to show his clan that he wouldnae be taken advantage of by the MacVales again, and nor would he trust us easily."

He took another step toward her. "After that, I looked forward to every trip I made to the MacDonnell keep, even when months passed between visits, and even when I kenned a cold reception awaited me. I didnae care, as long as I could catch a single glimpse of ye, or hear yer voice, or merely ken that ye were somewhere close by, under the same roof as I was."

"And...and the kiss we shared?"

His gaze was unwavering as he answered. "That was the best moment of my life."

A tempest of tangled emotions swirled within her. "I still dinnae understand, then. What changed between that kiss and now? One minute ye seemed to want me, and the next..."

Fillan's mouth compressed and a muscle ticked in his jaw. "Isnae it obvious?" He jerked his chin down toward his bad foot. "I didnae wish to saddle ye to a cripple for the rest of yer life."

He might as well have punched her in the stomach. "Fillan," she breathed. "How could ye think that ye... How could ye imagine that I would..."

But he seemed unconvinced by her half-formed protestations. He closed his eyes for a moment. "Ye dinnae understand what ye've been bound to. I cannae walk without a cane. I willnae ever be able to sweep ye up in my arms and carry ye to bed. If we were to ever have bairns, I couldnae play with them like a normal father. It is just as my father always said—I am damaged. I dinnae deserve ye."

Her heart shattered for him then. His father's brutality had left scars on the inside, even if the bruises and cuts had healed on the outside.

"That isnae what I see," she whispered. She met his gaze so that he could witness the truth of her words in her eyes. "I see a handsome man before me, one whom I have revered from afar these past three years. I see a Laird who was handed an impossible task and is somehow succeeding. One who has overcome a decades-long legacy of cruelty and dishonor in just three years, bringing prosperity and pride back to an entire clan. Who is protective of his people, clever, kind, and stead-fast. And..."

She faltered then, but she could not hold back the truth any longer. "And I see a man whom I have already given my heart to. I can only pray that he will have a care with it."

Suddenly, he sat down hard on the edge of the trunk

at the foot of the bed. His breath left him in a sharp exhale. "Ye cannae mean all that."

Adelaide lowered herself beside him. "Aye, I do."

He seized her hand, bringing it to his wildly thumping chest. "Yer heart will always be safe with me. And I hope ye will look after mine as well, for it already belongs to ye."

"I will," she replied, her eyes pricking and her voice thick with emotion. "Always."

He gave a shaky huff. "Bloody hell. I was such a fool. Can ye forgive me?"

"Aye, if ye'll forgive me, too, for I was just as wrong as ye."

"How did we misunderstand each other so greatly?" he mused.

"I suppose we both mistook the other to suit our own insecurities," she said, lowering her lashes. "Ye for thinking I couldnae care for ye, and me for believing ye didnae want me."

"I vow no' to jump to conclusions anymore, and to talk plainly with ye instead," he said.

But then he stilled, his face darkening with worry.

"I dinnae wish to hide aught from ye, Adelaide. So before we go any further in this marriage, ye should see what ye'll be dealing with if ye choose to stay."

CHAPTER 10

Trepidation flowed through Adelaide at Fillan's veiled words, but she nodded.

Fillan reached for the boot on his clubbed foot and began unlacing it. She watched, uncertain what he was about.

It took several tugs to pull the boot free, for he'd wedged the foot into it despite the fact that it wasn't made to accommodate the bend in his ankle. This close, she could see that the outside edge of the boot was worn down from where he walked on it.

When at last he'd removed the boot, he pulled himself to his feet with the use of his cane. She could see clearly now the way his foot curved inward. To walk, he had to put his weight on the edge of the foot, which was heavily callused and blistered from rubbing inside the boot. His calf was slimmer on that side as well.

"Does it hurt?" she murmured.

"Aye." His voice was tight with discomfort at being exposed to her stare, but he held still and let her look. "Mostly when I walk too much, but it also gets achy for no reason from time to time. But ye havenae seen all just yet."

He extended his hand to her, helping her rise from the trunk. Then he opened the lid and withdrew a frightening-looking contraption. It was a series of leather straps and wooden dowels. To her eye, it looked like some sort of torture device.

"This is my brace," he said, perching on the chest once more so that he could set aside his cane and use both hands. He held up the contraption. "My leg goes in here and my foot here. Then I tighten it so that it pulls my foot straight—well, as straight as I can stand it, for it hurts like the bloody devil."

Adelaide tried to hide her horror, yet she could not help but breathe, "Why inflict such a thing on yerself, then?"

Fillan slowly lowered the brace and placed it on the trunk's lid. "I dinnae like being this way, Adelaide. The brace is supposed to help. I only wear it at night, though, which makes my progress slow and painful."

"Why only at night?"

"A holdover from my father," he said softly. "He wouldnae let me wear a brace in front of others. He believed it was a sign of weakness."

Though it was unchristian to think such thoughts of the dead, Adelaide silently cursed Serlon MacVale for all the ways he'd hurt Fillan.

"He might have seen fit to correct my foot when I was but a wee newborn bairn," Fillan continued. "If he'd started me on the brace then, my foot might be straight now. But he wouldnae. No son of his would draw attention to such a flaw, cripple or nay, he used to say. I fashioned this brace myself a few years before his death and wore it in secret every night. It helps stretch my foot closer to straight during the night, but the day seems to take away all my progress."

"But…" She hesitated, trying to choose her words about this delicate topic carefully. "But yer father is gone now. Ye neednae live by his rules anymore. Why do ye still only wear the brace at night?"

Fillan released a long breath. "I am still my father's son. I dinnae like appearing enfeebled in front of my people. I want to be a better Laird to the clan—a strong Laird."

"But ye are—dinnae ye see?" She moved the brace out of the way so that she could sit beside him once more. "Ye have led them into a solid alliance with the Mackenzies. And soon, I hope ye can count on the MacDonnells as well. My father is stubborn, but he isnae blind. He and I both saw how much yer people respect ye. They are following yer lead in living with honor, working hard, and righting the wrongs of the past."

He lifted his gaze to her. Though his eyes still bore uncertainty, he took her hand and squeezed it. "Thank ye for saying that."

Feeling warm under his steady stare, she ducked her

head. Her eyes landed on his clubbed foot once more. Belatedly, she noticed that the dark hairs on his legs had been rubbed off and his skin was red and chafed where the brace's straps would lay.

He must have followed her gaze, for he said, "Since I only wear it for a few hours, I have to pull the straps tight, else the brace does little."

"Mayhap if ye wore it during the day as well, ye wouldnae have to tighten it so," she offered gently. Then she glanced at the brace, assessing it. "And ye could line the straps with something a wee bit softer. Linen, mayhap, or even silk." She looked up at him. "I could do that for ye."

"Nay, ye dinnae need to—"

She placed her palm over his heart, which made him go still. "I would never push ye to wear the brace during the day if ye dinnae wish to. Ye could stop wearing it all together and it wouldnae change how I feel about ye, nor how much yer people respect ye. But if ye continue wearing it, at least let me make it more comfortable for ye. I am yer wife now. I want to take care of ye."

Raw, unguarded emotion shimmered in the depths of his dark eyes. "Ye are a blessing, Adelaide."

But all too soon, his face clouded once more with uncertainty. "Does that mean...ye willnae seek a nunnery, then? Ye will stay with me as my wife? Ye can still leave if ye wish," he hurried on. "Since we havenae consummated, I wouldnae stand in yer way if ye want an annul—"

Impulsively, she rocked forward and stopped his words with a kiss. He froze for several heartbeats, but then his mouth melted against hers and his arms looped around her, drawing her to him.

Just like their first kiss, this one transformed slowly from tender to heated, deepening until their tongues caressed. Adelaide's pulse careened higher as his fingers sank into her back possessively.

Panting, Adelaide pulled back, breaking their kiss.

"What is wrong?" Fillan breathed, brushing a strand of hair from her cheek.

"I was wondering… That is, I hoped that we might make this a real marriage?" Her face felt as though it was on fire at the bold words. She waited a breathless moment while Fillan digested what she was saying. His brows lowering in confusion, then an instant later, his eyes widened and his lips parted.

"This is our wedding night, after all," she murmured, smiling shyly.

"I want naught more in the world," he replied. "But are ye sure? We neednae rush if ye dinnae want to."

"Oh aye." Now she blazed all over, but her embarrassment was laced with a kindling fire of desire. "I am verra sure."

Like lightning, he was on his feet, guiding her up after him with one hand and gripping his cane in the other so that he could walk her toward the edge of the bed. But instead of sitting, he released her hand and began tugging his shirt from his belted plaid.

Once it was over his head, she was gifted with the sight of his bare torso. Though he was not bulky with thick muscle, his shirt had hidden a lean, sinewy strength. Firelight danced over the hard planes of his chest and stomach, etching each distinct muscle with shadow.

He shifted his weight to his good leg and propped his cane against the bed so that both his hands were free to work on his belt. Once it popped free, he caught the plaid as it slid down his hips and draped it over the foot of the bed.

Belatedly, Adelaide realized she'd sunk onto the mattress, her legs no longer seeming to work properly.

After Euna had been married, she'd told Adelaide what happened between a man and a woman. Yet looking at all Fillan's masculine lines and angles, she wasn't sure if it would work. His manhood already jutted rigidly from his body. He seemed far too big, too hard for her to take.

"Dinnae be afraid." He must have easily read her face, for his voice was gentle as he moved to the bed. "We are made to be joined, sweeting. There will be some discomfort, but just this first time. After that, it will only be pleasure."

Euna had said the same thing. And if Fillan's kiss was any indication, there could be a great deal of pleasure between them.

He found the laces running down the back of her gown and began working them loose. When they were undone, she stood and shimmied the gown off her shoulders and down her hips. It puddled in a blue pool of wool at her feet. Standing in naught but her linen chemise, she hesitated, suddenly unsure.

"Ye never have need to be shy with me, Adelaide,"

Fillan said, gazing upon her reverently. "Ye are the most beautiful creature I have ever beheld."

Rising to his feet, he laid his hands on her shoulders and skimmed down her arms. His warm touch sent a ripple of gooseflesh over her skin. His hands moved to her waist, then her back, then her hips, always sliding light as a feather's caress.

It was almost as if he were afraid to touch her, like she would turn to mist beneath his hands if he pressed too firmly. He seemed to caress the material of her chemise more than he did her heated skin underneath, and the linen touched her in return. The sensation sent fiery tendrils of desire over her, making her shiver with longing.

He lowered his head toward her, but instead of kissing her lips, he brushed his mouth along her collarbone. He dropped a kiss into the rapidly pulsing hollow at her throat, then trailed upward until he reached her ear. By the time he flicked and nibbled the sensitive flesh there, a bonfire of need roared low in her belly.

And when he cupped her breasts in his hands, brushing his thumbs over the pearled peaks, a moan escaped her throat.

"Please," she breathed, though she wasn't sure what she was asking for. Relief from the torturous pleasure and more of it at the same time, she supposed distantly.

The chemise whispered over her heated skin as he pulled it up and over her head. She stood bare before him now. For one heartbeat, shyness once again prodded her to cover herself, but when she saw the look in Fillan's dark eyes—part awe, part fierce hunger—she held herself still.

"God in heaven," he muttered, drinking in the sight of her.

Suddenly no longer able to hold himself back, he drew her to the bed. Flicking back the covers, he eased her down. She shivered again at the feel of the cool sheets, but a heartbeat later, Fillan slid in beside her, his body as blazing hot as a forge.

His lips found hers and she melted into their kiss. She arched into his roaming hands, letting the building sensations chase away her nerves.

When one of his hands slid between her legs, she instinctively opened to him, trusting in the pleasure his touch would bring. And it did. She gasped as he slipped a finger into the dampness there, tracing around her entrance and over that bud of raw pleasure above it.

Her breaths grew ragged as he stroked and kissed her. The wild thud of her heart mixed with her moans in her ears, her body drawing taut as the pleasure mounted.

"Ready?" Fillan's low voice vibrated through her.

"Aye," she panted.

He moved over her, nestling between her thighs. He took himself in hand until he brushed her entrance. But once he was in position, his fingers returned to that delicious spot just above, circling slowly.

In response to her building need, she lifted her hips to him, inviting him in. He eased forward slowly, taking her inch by aching inch. Just as he'd warned, discomfort began to swell as he pushed deeper until she gasped in pain.

He stilled except for the hand between them, which continued to stroke and caress her until pleasure edged out pain and she was panting and moaning once more. As she relaxed, he pushed all the way inside, filling her, stretching her. Claiming her.

Slowly, he rocked out, then eased forward once again. As she caught his rhythm, she met his strokes. When she rolled her hips, he groaned, the muscles in his neck straining. Oh, she liked that. Liked the pleasure it brought them both, aye, but also liked to see him unravel, his restraint slipping, and all thanks to her.

He sped his thrusts then, and all thoughts of being in control fled. She felt as though she were climbing toward something, straining for the blinding heat of the sun. And then she reached it. Her pleasure expanded in a white-hot burst. She cried out, trembling and arching as she rode through the ecstasy.

Just as she began to descend from the heights of her release, Fillan's own pleasure exploded with shuddering force. He growled her name, holding himself deep before slumping over her.

Gently, Fillan eased himself beside her and pulled her into his embrace. They caught their breath in silence for a moment.

"That was…"

When she couldn't find the words to describe the powerful connection they'd just shared, Fillan finished for her.

"That was just the beginning," he murmured,

running his fingers along her bare arm. But when his hand stilled, she lifted her head and found his brows drawn seriously.

"Ye still think ye can be happy here…with me?"

"More than happy," she replied, smoothing his brow with a gentle hand. "For I get to have ye as my husband for all my days."

"Aye, wife," he said, his gaze steady and warm. "I am yers."

EPILOGUE

"I have a surprise for ye."

Fillan looked up from his writing desk, where he'd been penning a missive to Reid about the progress he'd made with Laird MacDonnell.

Adelaide stood in the doorway of their bedchamber, something held behind her back.

"Oh?"

Her soft eyes shone as she nudged the door closed with her foot and stepped toward him.

"Aye. A present of sorts."

He lifted a brow at her. "Yuletide was nigh on a month past, wife, and my birthday isnae for another several months still."

"Call it a belated wedding present, then," she replied, halting before him. Carefully, she drew a large bundle wrapped in wool from behind her back. She set it on the edge of the desk and lifted one corner of the wool to peer inside.

"This first," she said, reaching in.

He lifted a brow. "I get more than one wedding present?"

She laughed softly. "Well, this first one is more the delivery of a promise I made ye. Hold out yer hands."

He did as she bade. When she placed the item in his palms, he recognized it instantly, yet it was different than the last time he'd seen it.

The wood and leather of his brace was now lined with smooth, dark blue silk.

"That should help with the chafing," Adelaide said. "Once ye try it, I can modify or remove the silk wherever it doesnae suit ye, but I thought this was a good start."

Eager to test the silk against his skin, he shucked off his boots and slid the brace over his clubbed foot—truly slid, for the silk took away all the friction that had pained him before.

"It is perfect," he said, meeting her gaze.

She beamed at him, but then her smile faltered with uncertainty.

"Now for the other. This is yer real present, but dinnae feel beholden to use it. I only thought...well, ye'll see."

She drew two more items from the wool wrapping, holding them up for him.

At first glance, he took them as a normal pair of leather boots. But as he continued to look, he realized one of the boots was different than the other.

The one for his left foot looked regular enough. But

the right boot, the one that would go over his clubfoot, was shaped oddly.

"I had Tam the cobbler help me with this," Adelaide said hurriedly. "He made the toe box—and the entire foot-well, really—wider than usual to give yer foot more room. And he wrapped the sole up and around the side so that ye arenae walking on the edge of yer foot without some protection."

Sure enough, the boot was wider, and the tougher material of the sole extended up the outside of the foot-well.

"He also made the space for yer calf a bit roomier," she continued.

Confusion hit him at that, for his calf was slimmer on the right side than the left, but she hurried to explain.

"That way, if ye choose…that is, if ye wish to wear yer brace during the day…" She took a fortifying breath. "It was made so that ye can wear yer brace under it. That way, the clan willnae see it if ye dinnae wish them to."

He sat in stunned silence for a long moment, simply staring at the boot.

"As I said, ye dinnae have to use it. I can ask Tam to fashion ye another boot to match the left one. And if I have overstepped, I ask for yer—"

"I love ye."

They both blinked in surprise at his blurted reply. They hadn't spoken of love before, but it felt natural say the word now, for it had been growing within his heart for so long.

He recovered first. "I love ye," he said again. "And I

love them. This is the most thoughtful gift I have ever received."

"Then I havenae overstepped?" she asked tentatively. "Ye ken I dinnae care if ye wear the brace at night, during the day, over yer boot, or under it."

"Aye, I do."

"And ye love me?"

"Of course I do," he said, giving her a soft smile. "How could I no'?"

"I love ye, too." At the shy blush that stole over her cheeks, his heart swelled against his ribs.

"I cannae wait any longer to try this," he said, reaching for the boot. He loosened the laces and guided it over his foot and brace. It was no longer a struggle to angle his bent foot into the boot, and it easily encased the brace around his calf. He stood slowly. The brace gave him extra stability, but he used his cane to steady himself as well.

Gone was the pinching and pain from his old boots. The brace lay smoothly beneath the thick leather. Though his limp would still be evident, he wouldn't have to display the awkward contraption he wore under the boot if he didn't wish to.

"This is…absolutely perfect," he said, taking a few experimental steps. He fixed her with his gaze. "As are ye, my love."

She flushed again, this time with pride. "Tam did most of the work. I only made suggestions. I wasnae sure if ye would mind that I involved him, but he was honored and humbled at the prospect of helping his Laird."

"I will be sure to thank him later. But I think I must thank ye first."

Adelaide must have caught the gleam in his eyes, for her brows lifted and she gave a breathy chuckle. "But it is the middle of the day!"

"What does that matter?" He stalked forward, catching her around the waist and pulling her in for a kiss.

When he released her, she was breathless, her eyes smoldering with desire. Yet he hadn't quite won her over yet.

"Dinnae forget that my father is to arrive within the hour to discuss yer new trade agreement."

"Let him wait," he growled, leading her toward their bed. "My lady wife is far more in need of my attention."

She followed him willingly, her sweet laughter filling the room. When he reached the bed, he sat down on the edge, drinking in the bonny vision of her smiling face.

"Come here, my Yuletide bride, and let me show ye how much I love ye."

With another joyous laugh, she launched herself into his arms and they tumbled together, their limbs tangling and their hearts lifting as one.

The End

AUTHOR'S NOTE

As always, it is one of my great joys in writing historical romance to combine a fictional romantic storyline with real historical details. Plus, it's such a treat to share not only a thrilling, passionate, and emotional love story with you, lovely readers, but to give you a glimpse at my research into the history surrounding this book as well.

Before the Scottish Reformation of 1560, Christmas in Scotland was known as Yule. *Yule* is the Scot-ification of the Old Norse word *jól*, the word for their winter solstice festivities. Yuletide refers not just to Christmas day but the festive season associated with it, which began before Christmas and continued until after the new year.

Medieval Scottish Yule celebrations were a blend of Christian traditions and the pagan solstice festivities the Vikings brought with them to Scotland, some of which have stuck around to this day.

Evergreen boughs (an ancient version of the

Christmas tree) were brought inside to decorate hearths and rafters. They were meant to represent a celebration of the renewal of life on the darkest days of the year. Mistletoe was also hung overhead. Celtic peoples believed it had magical properties of healing, along with increasing fertility—hence all the kissing that happens beneath it! It was also used to ward off evil and bring good luck to those who passed under it.

Now a tasty dessert, the Yule log was traditionally an entire tree that was carefully selected and brought inside with great care. One end of the log would be fed into the fire slowly, as it was meant to last for the entire length of Yuletide. Part of the log was saved to light the following year's log. In between years, the log was kept around to ward off evil, illness, and bad fortune. The ashes of the Yule log were also saved for good luck.

In addition to evergreen boughs, mistletoe, and a yule log, a Yuletide celebration wasn't complete without a feast! Medieval feasts would have included mincemeat pies, goose, venison, honeyed bannocks, vegetables, puddings, and of course wine, ale, and mead—and probably some whisky.

Carols were also sung, but caroling in the medieval era was much different than today. Only one person would sing, accompanied by musicians if they were available, while the rest of the Yuletide revelers danced in a circle or linked chain. It wasn't until later in the medieval era that carol singers joined together and roamed from house to house, singing in exchange for small gifts. That was because singing carols was banned in churches (serious, somber Christmas masses were being disrupted with too much singing and dancing), so carolers were sent outside.

Moving on to some medieval wedding traditions, I had fun incorporating the throwing of the garter (another ritual that has survived to the modern day) into this story—though it has a rather shocking origin.

To ensure that the marriage was consummated, the priest, or sometimes family members of the bride and groom, would follow the newlyweds to their bedchamber and stay to watch. (There really was no such thing as privacy in the medieval era!)

The observer(s) would then take an undergarment of the bride's, like the garter, and present it to all those who'd attended the wedding as proof that consummation had taken place. The bride's clothes were considered good luck, so guests would scramble in hopes of grabbing the garter to keep for themselves.

Eventually, this practice of observing the consummation and taking the garter grew a bit too invasive for medieval couples. So the groom started removing the bride's garter and tossing it to the waiting guests before ducking away to consummate their vows in peace. It was also believed that if a husband could somehow retrieve the tossed garter and present it to his bride, then they would have a happy and faithful marriage.

A final note on my portrayal of Fillan's clubfoot. Clubfoot is a birth defect that occurs in one out of every one thousand newborns, affecting male babies about twice as often as females. One or both feet rotate inwards, and if it's not treated, a person will walk on the outside of his foot, creating a limp and walking problems.

Clubfoot was first depicted in ancient Egyptian tomb paintings. Treatments were described in India as early as 1000 B.C.E. Hippocrates wrote about using braces and special shoes to correct clubfoot at around 400 B.C.E.

In the modern era, people with clubfoot are treated from birth with surgery, or braces and casts that help straighten the foot and stretch the overly-tight ligaments pulling it inward. But in the medieval era, when physical deformity was considered a reflection of weakness of character or moral failing, fewer options were available. While braces were still sometimes used, often barber-surgeons and bonesetters applied overly harsh "remedies"—or the afflicted individual was simply left unaided to deal with their disability.

That was why it was so important to me to give Fillan (and Adelaide) a happily ever after. When both characters first appeared in *The Bastard Laird's Bride* (Highland Bodyguards, Book 6), I knew they would return for their own story, and their own happy ending.

Thank you for journeying back in time to medieval Scotland with me, and look for more riveting history and unforgettable romance in the tenth book in the Highland Bodyguards series, Will Sinclair's story, coming in 2019!

Make sure to sign up for my newsletter to hear about all my sales, giveaways, and new releases. Plus, get exclusive content like stories, excerpts, cover reveals, and more.

Sign up at www.EmmaPrinceBooks.com

THANK YOU!

Thank you for taking the time to read *The Laird's Yuletide Bride* (Highland Bodyguards, Book 9.5)!

And thank you in advance for sharing your enjoyment of this book (or my other books) with fellow readers by leaving a review on Amazon. Long or short, detailed or to the point, I read all reviews and greatly appreciate you for writing one!

TEASERS FOR EMMA PRINCE'S BOOKS

Highland Bodyguards Series:

Read Corinne and Reid's story and meet Fillan and Adelaide for the first time in **The Bastard Laird's Bride** (**Highland Bodyguards, Book 6**). Available now on Amazon.

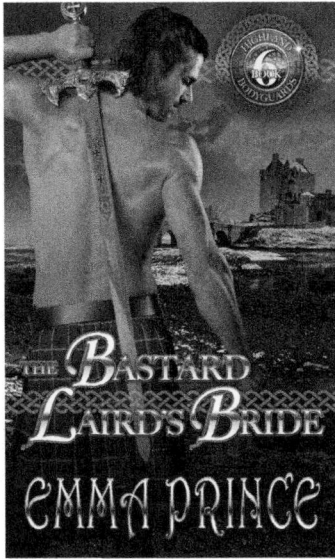

A forced marriage... A desire that can't be denied...

To thwart a marriage alliance, Laird Reid Mackenzie kidnaps an English noblewoman en route to her fiancé. But to Reid's horror, King Robert the Bruce orders that he now marry the bride he stole. With his legitimacy already in question, the last thing Reid needs is an English wife who will enrage his allies and embolden his enemies. Yet despite his opposition to marrying Corinne, her fiery spirit and matching beauty threaten to burn away his resistance and bring him to his knees with desire.

Corinne wants nothing more than to work as a scribe. With her wedding to a cruel fiancé looming, she decides to take matters into her own hands. But just when she initiates a daring escape, she is thrust into the arms of a dark Highland Laird whose stormy gaze leaves her breathless. Though she is desperate for freedom, her resolve begins to crumble under Reid's heated touch. As she struggles to make a home in the Highlands—and in Reid's heart—their union pushes the clan to the brink of war, forcing Reid and Corinne to choose between peace and their budding love.

The Highland Bodyguards Series continues with Niall and Mairin's story in *His Lass to Protect* (**Highland Bodyguards, Book 9**). Available now on Amazon.

To prove herself, she'll brave anything. To protect her, he'll risk everything.

As the only woman in King Robert the Bruce's Bodyguard Corps, Mairin Mackenzie is eager to prove herself. When the King proposes a mission to sow the seeds of civil war in England, Mairin jumps at the chance, even though returning there means confronting the nightmarish trauma of her past. But to her frustration, the Bruce decides to send a second bodyguard with her—Niall, the only Englishman in the Corps. Although Niall kindles a surprising heat within her, Mairin has sworn to hate the English until the day she dies. When she is faced with a chance at personal vengeance, can she trust in her strength, even if it means ignoring what's in her heart?

Niall Beaumore fears this mission will be his undoing. After six long years in the Bruce's Corps, this is his best chance to show how deep his allegiance to Scotland runs. Yet being paired with Mairin is far more dangerous than anything he's faced before. From the moment he laid eyes on her, Niall has been captivated by the fire behind Mairin's dove-gray gaze. After failing to protect those he cares about once before, he vows never to let Mairin come to harm. But when duty clashes with desire, they'll both be forced to choose between an unexpected love and the very fate of Scotland's freedom.

The Sinclair Brothers Trilogy:

Go back to where it all began—with Robert and Alwin's story in *Highlander's Ransom*, Book One of the Sinclair Brothers Trilogy. Available now on Amazon!

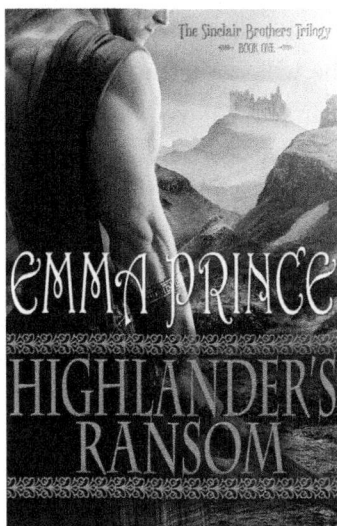

He was out for revenge...

Laird Robert Sinclair will stop at nothing to exact revenge on Lord Raef Warren, the English scoundrel who brought war to his doorstep and razed his lands and people. Leaving his clan in the Highlands to conduct covert attacks in the Borderlands, Robert lives to be a thorn in Warren's side. So when he finds a beautiful English lass on her way to marry Warren, he whisks her away to the Highlands with a plan to ransom her back to her dastardly fiancé.

She would not be controlled...

Lady Alwin Hewett had no idea when she left her father's manor to marry a man she'd never met that she would instead be kidnapped by a Highland rogue out for vengeance. But she refuses to be a pawn in any man's game. So when she learns that Robert has had them secretly wed, she will stop at nothing to regain her freedom. But her heart may have other plans...

Viking Lore Series:

Step into the lush, daring world of the Vikings with *Enthralled* (**Viking Lore, Book 1**)!

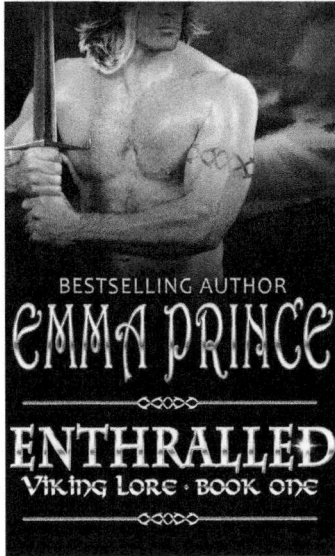

He is bound by honor...

Eirik is eager to plunder the treasures of the fabled lands to the west in order to secure the future of his village. The one thing he swears never to do is claim possession over another human being. But when he journeys across the North Sea to raid the holy houses of Northumbria, he encounters a dark-haired beauty, Laurel, who stirs him like no other. When his cruel cousin tries to take Laurel for himself, Eirik breaks his oath in an attempt to protect her. He claims her as his thrall. But can he claim her heart, or will Laurel fall prey to the devious schemes of his enemies?

She has the heart of a warrior...

Life as an orphan at Whitby Abbey hasn't been easy, but Laurel refuses to be bested by the backbreaking work and lecherous advances she must endure. When Viking raiders storm the abbey and take her captive, her strength may finally fail her—especially when she must face her fear of water at every turn. But under Eirik's gentle protection, she discovers a deeper bravery within herself—and a yearning for her golden-haired captor that she shouldn't harbor. Torn between securing her freedom or giving herself to her Viking master, will fate decide for her—and rip them apart forever?

ABOUT THE AUTHOR

Emma Prince is the Bestselling and Amazon All-Star Author of steamy historical romances jam-packed with adventure, conflict, and of course love!

Emma grew up in drizzly Seattle, but traded her rain boots for sunglasses when she and her husband moved to the eastern slopes of the Sierra Nevada. Emma spent several years in academia, both as a graduate student and an instructor of college-level English and Humanities courses. She always savored her "fun books"—normally historical romances—on breaks or vacations.

But as she began looking for the next chapter in her life, she wondered if perhaps her passion could turn into a career. Ever since then, she's been reading and writing books that celebrate happily ever afters!

Emma loves connecting with readers! Sign up for her newsletter and be the first to hear about the latest book news, flash sales, giveaways, and more—signing up is free and easy at www.EmmaPrinceBooks.com.

You can follow Emma on Twitter at: @EmmaPrince-Books. Or join her on Facebook at: www.facebook.com/EmmaPrinceBooks.

Printed in Great Britain
by Amazon

40084106R00067